PRAISE FOR
*The Icarus Gland*

*'The best science fiction writer in Russia'*

– New Horizons

# THE ICARUS GLAND

Books by Anna Starobinets translated into English:

*An Awkward Age*

*The Living*

Translation of this publication and the creation of its layout were carried out with the financial support of the Federal Agency for Press and Mass Communication under the federal target program "Culture of Russia (2012-2018)."

Published with the support of the Institute for Literary Translation (Russia)

AD VERBUM

ANNA STAROBINETS

# THE ICARUS GLAND

## AND OTHER STORIES OF METAMORPHOSIS

Translated by James Rann

SKYSCRAPER

The publishers would like to thank Sue Sabbagh
for her help with the translation of the lullaby in '*Shhmoochie*'

Published by Skyscraper Publications Limited
Talton Edge, Newbold on Stour, Warwickshire CV37 8TR
www.skyscraperpublications.com
First published 2014


Designed and typeset by Grace Fussell Studio
Printed by Latitude Press Ltd
ISBN-13: 978-0-9551810-5-4

ANNA STAROBINETS

# THE ICARUS GLAND

## AND OTHER STORIES OF METAMORPHOSIS

Translated by James Rann

# TABLE OF CONTENTS

The Icarus Gland ........ *13*

The City ........ *35*

The Seeing-Eye ........ *57*

The Parasite ........ *70*

The Border ........ *88*

Green Pastures ........ *97*

Shhmoochie ........ *110*

## THE ICARUS GLAND

It started with trivial little things. He would get held up at work, often until late, and however much you called him, you'd get 'number not in service,' even though, supposedly, he didn't take the metro. And at home, in the evenings – not every day, but still quite often – he would take his phone off into the far room or the bathroom and shut the door tight "so that Bunny doesn't get in the way when I'm on a work call". But Bunny had long since grown up and didn't get in the way of phone calls. He didn't get in the way at all. He sat in his room, at the computer, in fluffy headphones; he was thirteen... Time was, Bunny would always be interrupting, and wouldn't let you make a phone call or watch TV; he would charge into the bedroom at seven in the morning – he was cheerful and clingy, and constantly wanted them to go into his room and look at something entirely ordinary which for some reason he suddenly found thrilling. "Look at what I've done with my cosmonaut," "Look at my tigers hiding round the corner," "Look at me draw this yellow sun," "Look," "Look"... When they were busy or didn't want to go and look, or just ignored him for his own good, Bunny would get anxious and start to jump up and down on the spot. That's why they gave him the name Bunny. Now he didn't care whether they came and looked, he didn't jump up and down any more and he didn't tell them to come to his room, but the nickname still remained, as a reminder of everything they hadn't seen and never would...

"Don't bring Bunny into this," she said once, when he came out of the bathroom holding his phone. "What's Bunny got to do with it? You were clearly hiding from me in there."

In reply she expected a denial, irritation, for him to make a face, say something about her being paranoid; she wasn't being serious, she just said it, as a warm-up, more in the sense that he was neglecting his son, and neglecting her, that he was being distant basically – but he suddenly started blushing, like a child – first his ears, then his cheeks and his forehead. And only then did it come – the denial, the irritation, the look. She got scared.

When he had fallen asleep, she went on *socio* and wrote in the search bar, "I think my husband is cheating on me".

Other people had it exactly the same. The same "symptoms", the same fears and suspicions. And for some it was much worse: "I found a text from my husband's lover on his mobile", "I found a photo of a naked girl in his in-box", "I found condoms in his pocket." She felt better. Calmer somehow. She was not alone, and they'd deal with their shared problem together.

Plus, there was no proof yet that she had a problem.

...She read the advice of a psychologist. "If you think that your husband is cheating, don't be afraid of discussing this issue with him. You should speak calmly, with no hysterics, shouting or ultimatums, even if your worst suspicions are confirmed. Hysterics will only scare off your Man and drive him into the arms of his lover. Be smart. Don't get mad at him, be sympathetic. Infidelity is a sort of illness, but, fortunately, it's curable."

She didn't like this advice, it missed the point. After all, it's not a question of how to behave when "your suspicions are confirmed". It's a question of how to extract the truth from him. She entered another search: "How do you know if your husband is cheating?"

Immediately a *socio*-test popped up: "Is your husband cheating?" Only ten questions. In a fancy pink font. She answered all the questions quickly, with the exception of numbers five, seven and ten:

**1. How old are you?**
a) under 30 b) <u>**30 to 40**</u> c) over 40

**2. How old is he?**
a) under 35 b) <u>**35-45**</u> c) over 45

**3. Has he had the operation?**
a) yes b) <u>no</u>

**4. Do you have sex...**
a) more than once a week b) between once a week and once

every 2 weeks c) <u>less than once a week</u>

**5. Does he show you signs of affection?**
a) yes b) no

**6. Do you have children together?**
a) <u>yes</u> b) no

**7. Does he spend time with the children?**
*(Skip this question if you don't have children)*
a) yes b) no

**8. Does he often work late?**
a) <u>yes</u> b) no

**9. Does he spend weekends with the family?**
a) always b) <u>not always</u>

**10. Are you an attractive woman?**
a) yes b) no

Numbers five, seven and ten prompted doubts. Does he show signs of affection – what are you supposed to understand by that? Meaning, does he buy her flowers? Well, for her birthday at least. Does he help her on with her coat? Yes, of course, he's well brought up. Nice surprises, perfume, jewellery, cinema tickets? No, none of that… Although at the weekend he always brings her coffee in bed. With a little sandwich – he makes these delicious little sandwiches… It's nice. So, signs of affection – <u>yes</u>. But as for the others… Does he spend time with the children? That's not the right question. *You* try and spend time with Bunny. He's an independent, self-sufficient sort of Bunny. He's got his computer, his *socio*-games, an enormous friend-feed, he keeps himself occupied. If the question were "does he love" him, "does he take care" of him – then yes. Definitely. He really loves the boy. He was even on the school's parents committee, but then they suspended him… Because when it was arranged for all the boys in the class to go for the routine operation and he had to sign the permission form – just a formality – he refused and Bunny didn't go to the clinic. One mother, the most active on the committee, said that they were irresponsible egotists. Subjecting a child to risk because of some crazy ideas of theirs, or, perhaps, just because they were too tight, even for something as important as this. But money has got nothing to do with it! She knew: he didn't let Bunny got to the clinic because he was afraid. There was a minimal risk – a few tenths of a percent – that something might go wrong. All those stories about teenagers that afterwards *sleep all the time*. He didn't want that. He said: "I don't need a stuffed Bunny." At the end of the day, Bunny is pretty placid and mostly sits at home, all his friends are on *socio* night and day. So they weren't taking such a risk... So, basically, **yes**, then: he does spend time with his son.

She didn't like the last question at all. Is she attractive... from whose point of bloody view? Angry, she whacked the pink "**yes**" with the mouse. But as she did, she thought about the wrinkle – the vertical one, on the bridge of her nose. The very obvious one. But if she pumped it full of botox, it might get even worse, make her face look all wooden.

And the grey hairs at her temples. Every month she dyes the roots that have grown out with a Japanese dye, but he *knows*. Stupidly, she'd told him herself. If she hadn't mentioned it, he wouldn't have noticed.

The outcome of the test depressed her: "There is a chance that your husband really is cheating. Maybe he's having a midlife crisis. Nonetheless, you have a good chance of getting the upper hand on your rival and saving your marriage. Elective surgery is almost sure to solve all your problems."

She was rereading her result for a third time when she heard a noise. The quiet sob of his mobile phone. He'd got a text. At two in the morning.

Something shifted painfully inside her – it was as if someone had pulled sharply on a thread and the ball of ice tied to that thread had leapt from her stomach into her throat and back again.

She had extracted the phone from under his pillow an hour ago. Just in case. She'd taken a look at the inbox and the sent folder. She hadn't found anything suspicious. But now there was something there.

It's the phone company, she told herself. Just the phone company. Telling him he's run out of credit...

It wasn't the phone company. One new message from "Dovey".

Dovey? What on earth... There's a Bunny and now there's a Dovey... Maybe it's Bunny's teacher?

She poked at the hot buttons with stiff fingers. Open message.

"Are you asleep?" That's all. Just three words. And a question mark.

She wrote back: "No."

Delivered.

"What about her?"

The ball of ice jumped up again inside her and got stuck in her throat. It was entirely obvious. Entirely obvious. But for some reason she wrote back again. "She is asleep." To be certain – the words went round in her head. To be almost certain, to be absolutely, definitely certain...

"Call me?" Dovey said. "I miss you."

"Bitch," she wrote.

No hysterics?

No accusations?

...It didn't work. She went into the bedroom, turned on the light and chucked the phone right in his face. He woke up, shaggy-haired and puffy-faced, ridiculous, like in a French comedy. He shielded himself from the light and from her. For some reason he covered his stomach with the duvet.

"Why Dovey?!" she screeched. "Why Dovey, why?!

For some reason that seemed like the most important question. It was.

"Because... it's like, sort of... love. Lovey-dovey, you see..."

"I see. You're screwing her. You're screwing a bird."

The ball of ice, forcing back the sides of her throat, slid back down, and she, finally, started crying. He, meanwhile, pulled on his pants and trousers. With his back to her. As if he were shy. As if he had something there she hadn't seen before.

She said: Get out! He obediently started getting dressed.

He was already in the corridor when she caught up and grabbed hold of his jacket; he stayed.

No hysterics, she kept repeating to herself, no hysterics, no shouting, no ultimatums. They sat down in the kitchen, she even poured him some tea, as if everything were fine, they talked, she kept herself under control, asking calmly: when did it start? how often? how serious is it? So, do you really love her?....and me? me? what about me?

He answered:

"I love you too. In my own way."

'In my own way.' She knew him too well. A gentle sort. He just couldn't say 'no' to people.

"In your own way?" she asked hoarsely.

And then suddenly she flung – good reactions, he ducked – Bunny's blue mug. With the tea still in it, or whatever was in there. Broken shards flew all over the kitchen, sludgy brown liquid stained the wall with enigmatic Rorschach tests.

...Trite, readymade phrases, not her own, but tacky, from off the TV, crawled on to her tongue, like ants emerging from a rotten overturned tree-stump. You've ruined my whole life... All the years I've given you... I want that time back…

"Quiet… the boy," he said, sounding hunted.

Standing in the kitchen door was a sleepy Bunny. Barefoot. In just a T-shirt. Another batch of ants came pouring out. She didn't want them to, but they crept out all by themselves:

"You should have thought about the boy back then, you old lech. When you went and got yourself *that girl!*"

"Dad, are you…" Bunny said in a deep voice, before finishing in a childish squeak, "…leaving us?"

"His voice is breaking," she thought detachedly, but out loud she said:

"Well, come on then. Answer your son, *Dad*."

"Don't you dare…" – he whispered with white lips – "…bring him into this."

He jumped up, went into the corridor and started pulling on his jacket again; in silence, with shaking hands, he zipped it up, taking a long time, much longer than necessary.

She shouted:

"If you leave, don't come back."

And she shouted other things too.

And Bunny said:

"Why do we need him if he doesn't want to be with us."

Then she went to her bedroom to cry, while he talked to Bunny about something, standing in the doorway. Then he went. To *that girl* of his. To *her*. Where else could he be going at five in the morning? But he didn't take any of his things, just his phone and wallet.

She sent him a text: "You have to choose – her or us." There was no reply. Then she wrote again: "You will never get to see Bunny again." A reply came: "Julia, that is blackmail." Swallowing her snivelly tears, she typed: "What else can I do with you, you bastard?"

In the morning her mother rang, her faultless vulture instincts having sensed this fresh pain.

"What's happened? There's something up with your voice."

"Everything's fine," Julia said. Her mother didn't give in. She kept circling around, insisting, suggesting, pecking away, tightening her circles – until she hit the sore spot.

"It's Igor, isn't it?" She nonchalantly buried her beak in Julia's wound.

"Found himself a little dolly bird, has he?"

Weariness swelled up in her, she didn't have the strength to resist, and she told her everything.

"Now you've gone and done it," her mother said contentedly. "Well, if you'd treated me with respect..."

"What has this got to do with you?" Julia moaned. "My God, what on earth has this got to do with you?!"

"Because you should listen to your mother. And your mother told you that it's dangerous if they don't have the operation. And what's happened now? You and your 'personal freedoms' have really gone and done it. Where's that free person of yours gone gallivanting off to now? Now look at Arkady Germanovich..."

...Arkady Germanovich, Julia's step-father, was no longer young, and somewhat worn, with stomach ulcers, when her mother inherited him, but he had been wonderfully operated on. He and her mother had worked hard to build a three-room nest in a residential area, and deep down he wasn't a bad guy, but Julia didn't like him because he made stupid jokes and his breath smelled rotten.

"...and you'd have lived together happy as you like... but now you'll rue the day you didn't listen to your mother in time... you have to do the right thing... look after the boy... before it's too late... what if something happens... you're hurting your son... mark my words... sort it out ASAP... don't put it off... I know a wonderful doctor... a real genius..."

Julia hung up.

It was Saturday. Not a peep from him. She'd tried to call – not in service, her texts didn't get through. She spent the whole day as if she were in a murky fish tank. She didn't give Bunny anything to eat, so he clattered away with something in the kitchen himself. She sat on *socio*. She read about unfaithful husbands, about divorce and about the gland. She registered herself on the glandtidings.org forum, sketched out the situation and asked for advice. The people on the forum proved responsive – they threw together heaps of helpful links, and advised her, to a woman, to 'get it cut out asap'.

**Julia-Julia:** but he's left!! – she wrote in despair.
**k1ss3s:** hell b back wherez he gunna go
**nicksmum:** you ve got to think positive anyway you ve got a kid
**fairy33:** definatly if theres a little 1 they always come back!
**happy_goat:** ive pmed u the number of a clinic. even if he dont come back

☹☹ go along neway and take a look cos ule lern sumthin

He came that evening. Bunny didn't say hello and slammed his bedroom door. Igor smelled of tobacco and spirits, and of some strange, affectionate bitch. She wanted to hold him, hold him long and tight, to press the damp armpits of his shirt against him, and her hair and her mouth, to drown out this abnormal smell and mark him with her own scent, the smell of home.

Of course, she didn't touch him. She asked him tiredly:

"Why are you here?"

He said:

"Because I've chosen."

"Who?" she asked, already anticipating, already celebrating.

"You and Bunny," he said, like a schoolboy answering a question in class.

He was sick all evening: he had drunk too much and mixed his drinks; Bunny came over and asked in a wavering voice, how you doing, Dad?; she asked too and scratched on the door to offer to help. At the same time, automatically, she listened in to check whether he was on the phone.

When he felt better and Bunny had turned out his light, they sat in the kitchen to talk. He begged for forgiveness. He said that the family meant everything to him. Promised that he wouldn't cheat.

She listened with a special "bored" face. Then she said:

"I don't believe you."

"Why not?"

"Yesterday you said you loved someone else."

"I'll get over it eventually."

She was furious. That was the wrong answer.

"It's nothing serious," he corrected himself obediently. "I love you. You and Bunny."

She sat on his lap.

They sat there for a long time, like before, as they had long ago. She said:

"I just have one condition."

❧ ❧

"...The operation? What a load of rubbish! I don't need surgery. I'm not a little boy. I'll decide for myself. And it is my decision, I think. Just stop it would you, I'm not going to stray! Not in a year's time either. I am in control of myself. Don't try and twist things. No, I am not torn! No, I haven't called her. But I know that I haven't. Go on then, please, you can look on my phone. I haven't deleted anything. I never delete anything! Go snooping through my email if you like. It's a normal word. I haven't deleted anything. We're not in contact. No. I'm not hiding anything. What's the point of all this?! Julia, darling, what's the point of this operation? I'm here, I'm home. Julia, I'm with you even *without* it. I don't understand. No, I really don't understand. 'To be on the safe side'?! Do you even know how dangerous it is? At my age… Are you willing to put me at risk?! Harmless? Where does it say that? On *socio*?! You go back on that *socio* of yours! And what if it says on there that I should jump out the window? No, I don't want to take a look…!"

She made him read an article on Glandtidings. A very smart, sensible article, written, incidentally, by an expert. They read it together: he snorted indignantly; she felt almost normal.

She'll persuade him. She'll make him. Blackmail, tears – it doesn't matter, it's all for the best, for Bunny, for the family, for him.

Everything will work out.

He will atone for his sins.

She will forgive and forget.

The main thing is to find a good clinic.

www.**glandtidings**.net

Removal of the Icarus Gland: Myths and Realities

The Icarus gland is an endocrine gland present in humans and some animals. In humans the Icarus gland is small in size (not more than 2cm across) and located near the solar plexus. It is a ***vestigial organ***. In women the gland is practically atrophied, with the remaining fragments having fused to the upper ***mesenteric lymph node*** and the nerves leading from it. In men the gland is still preserved as an independent organ. This gland begins producing ***hormones*** in boys aged 11-12 and continues to do so until 60-65 years. The hormones made by the Icarus gland do not play a role in metabolism or help important organs to function. But the secretions of the Icarus gland do often have a negative effect on men's ***psychological make-up*** and ***temperament***. Doctors recommend that all males have this organ removed. A ***routine operation*** to remove the glands can be carried out at both state and private clinics.

At our clinic the operation is inexpensive and carried out by qualified doctors.

Unfortunately the general population is badly informed about the operation and idle speculation often leads people to put off a visit to the clinic until the situation becomes critical. To that end, we would like to list some of the basic facts about the operation.

OK. Fact No. 1

In animals the Icarus gland performs important functions. A release of the hormone produced by the gland into the blood of a predator (wolves, vixens, tigers etc.) triggers the so-called ***stalking instinct***, which helps them track and pursue their victims and also causes a specific ***blood thirst*** immediately before an attack.

It has been recorded that in migratory birds the highest concentrations of hormone are observed during seasonal migrations: evidence suggests that the gland helps birds keep their bearings in the air when flying across large bodies of water or during the hours of darkness.

A gland similar to the Icarus gland is found in the majority of insects that go through full cycles of transformation (for instance, ***neuroptera***) – it helps them to go through ***metamorphosis***.

Fact No. 2

In humans the Icarus gland is completely USELESS. Think about it: humans do not need to hunt prey and then tear it apart with their teeth and claws, humans don't fly over the sea at night and they don't pupate ☺

Fact No. 3

In humans a functioning Icarus gland is DANGEROUS. In teenagers the hormone that it produces can cause: aggressive outbursts, surges in adrenalin, unmotivated predisposition to risk, highly emotional and suicidal moods and various other psychological disturbances. In adult males – predisposition to weapon-use, risk-taking, vagrancy, drug dependency and marital infidelity. In unoperated men aged 35-40 a specific "midlife crisis" is frequently observed.

Fact No. 4

In many countries – for example, in the EU – removal of the Icarus gland is a compulsory operation undergone by all males.

Fact No. 5

In this country the operation is voluntary and is performed on the basis of a declaration (minors require the written consent of both parents). However, it should be noted, there are significant limits to the career opportunities open to unoperated males. A man with a functioning Icarus gland can never become a politician, doctor, teacher, or law-enforcement officer etc.

Fact No. 6

The Icarus gland can be removed from males aged 10 to 60.

Fact No. 7

The operation has no impact on men's health, or on their sexual and reproductive capabilities.

Fact No. 8

A routine removal of the Icarus gland will help preserve marriages, find peaceful resolutions to geopolitical conflicts and encourage nuclear disarmament ☺

and widespread myths (collected from monitoring ***socio***-forums)

Myth No. 1

"Without my Icarus gland I'll become lazy, fat, stupid and uninquisitive, I'll just eat and sleep."

That can happen with the gland too ☺ - there's plenty of examples. It has been statistically proven that post-op men not only do not lose interest in life, but are in fact more driven, more conscientious and more focused on success and career development than peers who are still dependent on surges of hormones.

Myth No. 2

"Without the Icarus gland I'll lose interest in sex."

See Fact No. 2. Sex drive does not suffer in any way. A healthy man will feel and fulfil the need for regular sex with his spouse.

Myth No. 3

"If my husband has his Icarus gland removed, he'll no longer be capable of loving me and he'll fall out of love with me immediately."

Nothing of the sort. Marital love is a sort of reflex – it is located in the brain and the operation has no effect on it whatsoever. On the contrary, the operation will probably protect you from your husband cheating or going on long business trips.

Myth No. 3

"After the operation my husband's personality will change for the worse. He'll take revenge on me for convincing him to remove the gland and will turn aggressive."

A man will not take revenge on you for making his life calmer and simpler. As a rule, the personalities of post-op men do not change, and if they do then it will be for the better. Men become more domestic and thoughtful and show more care for their homes and children, as well as more interest in cooking, television, interactive ***socio***-journeys and

***socio***-games.

Myth No. 4

"Removing the Icarus gland is a sin. I heard that the Icarus gland is effectively your soul. If it's removed, then when a person dies their soul doesn't go to heaven."

These are anti-scientific superstitions spread by members of the Icarian Brotherhood cult. In actual fact the Icarus gland has no connection whatsoever to religious belief or the afterlife. It has nothing to do with the "soul" either. Think about it: the gland, if it's not removed, dies along with the body and stays inside it, and doesn't ascend to the heavens (ask a coroner ☺).

What is more, the presence of the Icarus gland in many bloodthirsty creatures (jackals, wolves, hyenas), as well as ruthless ones (wolverines, dragonflies) and just plain nasty ones (caterpillars) disproves beyond any doubt the absurd Icarian theory of "the gland as a divine spark".

We note that in developed, civilised countries like Britain and France the Icarian Brotherhood is an illegal cult.

Myth No. 5

"There are often complications after this operation."

No. The operation to remove the Icarus gland is a simple one and in 99.9% of cases it is carried out without any complications.

Myth No. 6

"I'm afraid of getting the gland removed because it will hurt."

The operation is completely painless. What is more, the procedure is non-invasive and does not require open abdominal surgery. The doctor irradiates the Icarus gland for a few minutes with a special ray (all that you need to do is strip to the waist to expose the area around the solar plexus). Then, over the course of three (3) days the Icarus gland dies off by itself. The process is not reversible. During this period the post-op patient needs ***special care*** (see the "post-operative care" section).

Myth No. 7

"My neighbour/brother/father-in-law had his gland cut out and he still cheats on his wife anyway. So that must mean the gland can grow back?!"

No it doesn't. The Icarus gland NEVER recovers. In extremely rare cases after the operation some "living" fragments of the gland can remain in the solar plexus, which then have to be removed again. This only happens when the operation is carried out by an underqualified doctor. There have been no such incidents at our clinic.

It was a simple decision. Sad and simple. After two days he broke. He called *her,* he couldn't resist. He told Julia that he was going for a smoke on the stairs. She didn't smoke, but a minute later she went out to join him. She could sense it.

She didn't interrupt him, convinced that he knew that she knew, and she retreated. He returned, looking beaten.

He said it himself: "OK."

They decided to tell Bunny later, after it had been done.

The clinic was nice and clean and tidy and the staff were all smiley. The two of them waited in the corridor, flicking through magazines; opposite them were a young couple and a teenager accompanied by his mother. The young couple kept giggling at each other and kissing with a hearty smack. They're probably engaged: lots of people have the op before their wedding.

The teenager sat there slouching and messed about on his *socio*-pod. The expression on his face said something like "I couldn't care less", but his legs, if you looked closely, were shaking. The mother was flicking through The Good Housekeeper.

Igor was white and silent, gripping the arms of his chair as if he were on a plane and that plane were falling.

At last, they were called. It turned out they had to go and see the psychologist first. They went in together. The psychologist had a plastic smile and didn't look them in the eye.

"Do you have any questions?" he asked the bridge of Julia's nose.

She didn't actually have any questions. Out of politeness and a sense of due process she asked whether it would have any effect on Igor's health or ability to work.

"It'll have no effect whatsoever," the psychologist answered animatedly, with beads of boredom flashing in his eyes. "On the contrary. For me personally, after the operation I started getting fewer colds. And I don't get tired so often. Basically, I have no complaints when it comes to my health!"

She took a look at his doll-like face, content and healthy, then examined his figure impolitely: well-built, but not fat. He hadn't run to fat.

"The metabolism doesn't suffer in the slightest." The psychologist intercepted her gaze. "And you, Igor, why so quiet?"

"I haven't got any questions. I'll sign whatever I have to," said Igor, colourlessly.

"O-o-o-h, come come now." The psychologist wagged his finger jollily. "You sound as if you're about to sign your will! Right then… Julia, yes? Right then, Julia my dear, you pop out for a second and wait in the corridor while your husband and I have a little chat, man to man."

She got up, scared – God forbid it's all going to be called off? – but the psychologist was a sensible fellow. He gave her an imperceptible little wink, as if to say 'don't worry, I won't spoil anything.' She left.

The psychologist paused then confidentially, respectfully even, asked:

"So, was it an affair?"

Igor nodded.

"And your wife insisted? On the op?"

He nodded again. And added:

"We've got Bunny, you see…"

The psychologist tensed in incomprehension.

"…Erm, that's what we call our son."

"I see." The psychologist shook his head disapprovingly. "And if you don't have the surgery, you won't get to see the boy, right?"

"Right."

"A typical bit of manipulation. Not good."

A shiver of hope: is he really going to advise me not to have it removed…?

"And what about her, the other one?"

"The other one" – Igor closed his eyes tiredly – "said: come and live with me, I'll give you ten kids… And never make you go under the knife."

"'Under the knife' – what does that mean?" The psychologist furrowed his brow in incomprehension, which made him look like a very clever monkey.

"She was talking about the operation."

"Ah so that's it…" His face smoothed over for a moment. "Well, we don't use knives! Where do all these old wives' tales come from? Our procedure is non-invasive…"

He fell silent, looking with interest at Igor's forehead. As if trying to find traces of a lobotomy.

"Manipulation," he said finally. "From the both of them: manipulation. You are not free. You, Igor, are not a free man. You're dependent on hysterical women, on your gland, on hormones. Hormones and women decide everything for you. Isn't it time you freed yourself?"

"But will I really…" Igor shook his head to get rid of the intrusive gaze from his forehead. "But will I really be able to choose after *it*?"

"It's only after *it* that you will really be able to choose. Decide what you want for yourself." He held out the form to the client. "Fill it in in the corridor."

"Thank you, goodbye." The client scampered fussily towards the door, like a hen.

"Puppets," the psychologist thought as he watched him leave. "Limited, restricted people. Going grey at the temples and only now do they come to have it removed."

---

He managed to walk home by himself, and even drank a little water – giving him lunch wasn't allowed – but then he said:

"I think… I'm going to have a little lie-down."

He lay on his back and stayed lying there.

She knew that this would happen and that there was no point in being frightened. The doctor had given her precise instructions, written it all down on a piece of paper, and just to be sure she went on *socio* again.

For the three days while the gland is dying off, he will lie motionless on his back. This is the body's normal reaction to a change in the hormone profile. His eyes will be open. He will not be able to blink.

*moisten the conjunctiva of the eye with "artificial teardrops"*

*every 1.5 to 2 hours*

*the lighting in the room should be low*

He will be cold

*cover the patient well, put a hot water bottle at his feet*

He will need liquids

*in order to avoid dehydration feed him boiled water from a syringe,*

*every 2-3 hours*

He will be incontinent

*for evacuation of the bladder and bowels use adult nappies;*

*change them at least 1-2 times a day*

She did everything according to the instructions, very responsibly.

"Has he died or something?!" Bunny came back from lessons. "Has Dad died? Has my dad died?"

He turned on the light and looked into his wide-open glassy-blue eyes and his chin shook slightly.

"What are you on about…?" She smiled and clicked the switch.

*the lighting in the room should be low*

"...He's just had an operation..."

"An operation... *that* operation?" Automatically Bunny crossed his arms over his stomach. "The one he didn't want?"

"We decided," she said, emphasising the we, "that it would be better that way. The operation is harmless..."

Bunny didn't hear her out, but went off to his room.

She did everything the instructions said, for all three days, but Bunny didn't help. He sat on *socio*, munching crisps, only came out to go to the toilet and didn't look at her.

On the third day they ran into each other in the kitchen. She said:

"Bunny, you could at least say hello..."

He said "hlo" through gritted teeth, spat right into the sink with unwashed dishes in it and went off to his room.

On the third day Igor came to.

He groaned, tried to get up, vomited and fell back down, closed his eyes and fell asleep; she cleaned it all up.

An hour later he got out of bed and wandered off somewhere; his eyes were bloodshot, he didn't recognise her, said nothing and staggered around like a drunk. Bunny came out and watched this – biting his lip, not breathing – then bolted into the corner and whimpered gently. She wanted to comfort him; he waved his hand and squeaked "Go away".

They heard a noise – as if something had fallen in the bathroom – and she and Bunny ran in and found him, sleeping, on the floor. They dragged him back to the bedroom. Laid him down, covered him.

Bunny said calmly:

"What have you done to him."

But in theory, all this was entirely normal, it was just as bad for other people. Because on *socio*...

**nicksmum:** they have a hard time getting over it. mine wobbled about the place, puked, walked in his sleep. what he got up to at night I cant even say!
but then in the morning he was fresh as a daisy!
**happy_goat:** as soon as they wake up they have a bad time of it. they need care, warmth. ladies, love your men! show them tenderness and consideration, specially on the third night. and everything will be OK!
**k1ss3s:** the 3rd night is awful. dont let them near the windows!! and check on there breathing.

The doctor had also warned her about the third night. A standard psychotic disorder: *they want to go down as low as possible*. The instinct for self-preservation doesn't work. So you've got to close all the windows and balconies, block them off so he doesn't jump out... And if you live in a house, not a flat, then he might go and sleep on the ground, which is also dangerous: it's not exactly the month of May out there right now, frostbite, the kidneys, the prostate, well, you understand... She understood, but they lived in a flat, not a house. On the ninth floor. She blocked off the balcony with stools, one on top of another, so they would clatter over if he tried to get near the balcony. She shuttered all the windows, and hung little bells on all the catches, even in Bunny's room.

She decided not to sleep. But it looked as if he was snoring away so nicely, rhythmically, comfortably, and that comfort lulled her...

She woke up at the sound of a crash, and ran barefoot into the living room – sure enough, the stools!

He was on the balcony. He wasn't going to jump, no: he was looking down, hanging his head.

"What are you doing out here?" she shouted. "Igor, darling, Igor, for God's sake, what are you doing out here?!"

He came to, as if he had just woken up. He looked at her in surprise. He shuffled obediently to the bedroom, lay down and fell asleep at once.

Bunny appeared, and in a whisper either asked or explained:

"He wanted to kill himself."

She was furious, trying not to wake him, she hissed:

"What a load of rubbish?! I told you, they want to go down. That's how they react to the surgery..."

"You're lying."

"You... what's that...? Is that how you're going to speak to your mother...?"

Bunny left. She was disgusted to realise that she had talked about herself in the third person. In that same horrible folksy manner as her own mother. Mother Earth. The Holy Mother. The Great Mother.

Again, heavily, as if earth were being sprinkled on her from above, she started to be swallowed up by sleep. With great effort she clambered out, as if from a freshly dug grave, and then didn't go to sleep again. What if he goes on to the balcony again? Or the window? And then on that third night they get apnoea too. Their breathing stops.

*they just forget to breathe – you know, like babies*

She listened carefully. But his breathing was measured and even. And he didn't jump up again.

In the morning he started to recognise people, and to talk. That is, he didn't say anything, but if you asked him: Igor, dear, do you recognise me? he'd say: of course, you're Julia.

"And who is this?"

"That's Bunny."

She felt calmer immediately. But Bunny, for some reason, started crying.

Then, for many days, things were bad.

If he wasn't sleeping, then he'd sit for hours and hours staring at the wall. When you told him: get up, go and sit somewhere else, he would get up and sit somewhere else. If you told him to eat something, he'd eat it all up. Hug! And he'd hug. If you didn't say anything, he didn't move a muscle.

They would turn on the television and it seemed as if he was watching it. But if you turned it off, he would continue watching the dark screen, as if it made no difference.

Bunny would sit next to him and take him by the arm, but then he stopped. He said once, rudely, meanly:

"Why should I sit with him? You've as good as killed him."

Even she realised it: something wasn't right. Something had gone wrong.

She went on *socio*: "husband has changed after removal of gland" and suddenly all sorts of things came up… She hadn't seen this before. She hadn't read about this, she didn't know about it. She had used different search terms before…

**tatusik:** we got the op and now the whole family regrets it. he has become sort of mindless. he sleeps and eats the whole time.
**vampiress:** help! my son isnt recovering after a routine operation.
he is weak all over and apathetic and completely depressed.
he keeps saying I dont want anything.
**unknown user:** girls, take my advice, dont ever do it!! without the gland my husband has got mean and aggressive. all day he shouts at me and the kids. he pisses on the loo seat on purpose.

No, he hasn't become aggressive. Not the slightest bit of aggression. But apathy, indifference – for sure.

*sleeps and eats*

*I don't want anything*

Is that really what's going to happen?!

She bought a DVD of a sad, touching film, by his favourite director. He watched it attentively.

"Did you like it?"

"Yes."

"What did you like about it?"

"The acting. The writing."

She got down on her knees in front of him. She took his face in her hands.

"Forgive me…"

It was as if he didn't understand:

"For what?"

"For what I did to you."

"Oh, it's nothing. It doesn't hurt anymore."

"What, did it hurt?" She touched his stomach where his gland had been.

"Of course it hurt."

"We've got cocodamol and nurofen… Why didn't you say that it hurt?"

"I did."

She suddenly felt a pang above her belly button. By her solar plexus. Where the atrophied remnants had fused with the nerves…

She was so ashamed, so sorry for him, it was beyond repair, that she was ready to do anything. Even let him go. Give him back to *her*, to that snake, if that would help. It does happen after all. They do write, they write that "after the operation he cheated anyway"… She'd also read that sometimes it grows back all the same. And maybe – and actually this might well be the case – there are still some *fragments* there. Living fragments – and if she just gives him a chance, then maybe he'll warm up a bit, he'll get over it…

She phoned the doctor – he said, don't worry, wait, it will sort itself out.

She couldn't wait. She couldn't look at him, sitting there, holding a newspaper for an hour or two, and *not turning the pages*.

She took his phone – out of battery, turned off, just like him – she charged it, turned it on. Found her number. Dovey. As in Lovey. I hope you choke on your own feathers, birdbrain…

She called her.

"Yes?!" *She* picked up straightaway; her voice was fresh and clear.

Not feeling her lips, not feeling her tongue, she introduced herself, said that Igor wasn't well. Said – you can come and take him, I'll let him go, if that's what he wants.

"When should I come over?" asked this Dove, presumptuously, as if she were making arrangements with his secretary.

"Today, if possible."

She came the same evening.

So young – God, she's nineteen! – and so overdressed. As if she were going to the theatre. A plunging neckline, some black number, figure-hugging, glossy, skimpy. A funny little face, like a furry little animal with big eyes. And that neck. Such a long neck.

She had no idea what to do with her.

"Please, do come on in…"

She offered her a seat at the table.

They sat in silence, as if at a wake, all four of them. There were some nibbles: ham, sausage and cheese. No one ate, except for Igor. He didn't look at either of them.

But Dovey looked at him, at him - and you could see her heart beating under that skin-tight top.

"Would you like some coffee?" Bunny said in a deep voice.

Julia shuddered. She had forgotten about him.

But Bunny – her Bunny was sitting there, it turns out, all red, and devouring this Dovey with his eyes. Staring at the chain with a cross on it that snuck down into her cleavage. And her neck. And her firm nipples beneath the tight black number.

"So then, are you going to go with her?" she asked her husband while Bunny was messing about in the kitchen.

"Go where?"

She quipped bitingly:

"Forgotten the address, have you?"

"Let's go, hey, Igor, let's go…?" Like a siren song. Like a love spell. Like a lullaby. That voice, quiet and silky - it promised him life. It promised him sweat, and a loud thumping in the chest, and a bitter tang on his tongue, and pungent ooze, and a hot womanly embrace. She knew, his wife knew, what he was being offered. She thought in horror: he's about to say yes.

Bunny came back with the coffee cups.

"I'm not going," said Igor. "Sorry. My place is with my family."

She looked into that beloved, wooden face and tried to feel shame, as she had before, and not this gloating tickle of victory.

And *she* left, dressed so fancy, this slender little bird, and Bunny gave her a packet of tissues to take with her.

Then he came back to the table and said:

"I hate you both."

And then, all of a sudden, things sorted themselves out. Something like two days later, starting that Saturday.

She woke up in the morning – and he had brought her coffee. And a little toasted sandwich with tomato and cheese.

He waited for her to finish eating and drinking, and crawled in next to her under the duvet.

"Do you want to be on top or shall I?"

She said:

"First you, then me."

...And he didn't sit staring at a fixed point anymore, and he washed all the dishes. And then after lunch they watched a TV show about vampires together, and got scared and laughed.

But Bunny – only out of stubbornness, only so he wouldn't have to admit she was right – kept repeating that nothing had got sorted. That he was still "fake" and "dead".

Igor didn't take offence. He jokily goggled his eyes, hung out his soft tongue, and lisped in a scary voice:

"I'm a zombie, I'm a zombie..."

Bunny didn't like it. He got angry and left.

In the middle of the night he came back covered in blood and drunk.

"Now you've gone and done it!" Julia sighed.

She broached the subject gradually, in a roundabout way. By suggesting that something's not right with the boy. An awkward age. And, maybe, still... We should consider... A routine... because...

She was afraid to finish. She was afraid of how he'd react.

But he reacted wonderfully.

"He's got to have the op." He said it himself! "Otherwise who knows what will happen? It's not easy with the gland. Especially at his age."

They booked an appointment for two days later. They told Bunny while he was still hung over.

He squealed and thrashed: I don't want the operation! He tried, completely naked, to run away. He called someone, begged someone, grabbed at knives and forks. Oh God, oh Lord, they'd obviously let him run wild completely... How long has he been in this state...? It's lucky he's still alive. No, there's no time to waste. Get it out, ASAP...! They moved the appointment forward to the next day.

They had to lock Bunny in his room for the night. Harsh, but for the best. Because he'd gone a bit crazy and could very easily just run off, who knows where, into the night.

She was terribly tired. Bags under eyes.

"You go and get some sleep," Igor said.

She went. Barely able to put one foot in front of the other.

He was sitting in the living room; he had turned on the laptop and gone on a *socio*-journey to Africa. Bunny banged on the door – his room was off the living room – and shouted that he needed the toilet.

"You've got a pot in there," Igor said.

He had a little dig through the remains of ancient *hominids*, had a bit of a wander about, pressed on *Welwitschia*, a plant endemic to the Namib Desert.

*it grows two enormous leaves for the entire duration of its life (more than 1000 years) – socio* explained

*the roots go up to 3m deep; the plant can survive in arid conditions, using dew or fog*

*as a source of moisture*

"Open the door!" Bunny yelled. "Open the door, open up, open up!"

Igor liked the *welwitschia*. It was like a bird with two big wings.

"...If you don't open it I'll jump out the window!"

...Igor watched Berber women weaving colourful carpets... Manipulation.

"I'll jump, I swear!"

Primitive manipulation...

In Bunny's room the window opened with a crack; a bell tinkled briefly. Then everything went quiet.

I shouldn't open the door, Igor decided. If you open it, he'll run away again. He won't have jumped. He's probably hiding somewhere. He's waiting for me to open the door. He'll start yelling again in a minute.

But Bunny didn't yell anymore.

I should go and check, Igor thought. But the balcony in the living room doesn't face the right direction, I won't be able to see. I'd have to go outside. It's cold outside. Get dressed, zip up, go downstairs, walk round the building... Can't be bothered, plus it's cold.

He decided not to go.

After all Bunny was probably only sleeping.

## THE CITY

E*verybody Wants to Get to the City...*

...The neon words on the façade opposite burn so brightly that it hurts to look at them. You can try and block them out with the blinds, but it doesn't help. Because, when I close my eyes, I see those words imprinted on my retina, scorched red on black on the inside of my eyelids. "Everybody wants to get to the City. Not everyone manages. You did."

At night I barely sleep. It's too stuffy, too noisy, too bright. And my skin itches all over. Translucent gnats crawl through the torn mosquito net. When they have sucked their fill of blood, they turn a dark crimson colour. If you kill them, they burst like poisonous berries. It leaves shapeless brown marks on the wall.

The blinds are broken, you can't shut them fully. Through the dirty window panes, through the long gaps where slats have broken off, this city soaks into the room with a poisonous, unctuous radiance. It spreads shiny, greasy stripes on the walls and the sheets, on the pillow, on my face. It thunders with music, roars with motors and fire engine sirens. There's a lot of fire engines, day and night – why, I wonder? I've never seen a fire in the City. But they're constantly patrolling up and down the city streets, howling and spinning their cyclopean eyes, creating a sense of imminent disaster. The blinds reply to the sirens with tinny jangling.

At night I watch the glowing stripes on the wall and scratch myself terribly. The marks left by the gnats look like love bites.

This city has latched on to me and it's kissing me with its greedy, blood-stained proboscis.

When I had Sasha alongside me, it was easier to bear. She would place her kisses over the kisses of the City. She would kiss the bites to make them itch less. But now she's gone.

Everybody wants to get to the City. Get a job, emigrate, come for a week-end mini-break, take part in some cultural exchange, win a City-coupon, fly via the City then fall asleep in the airport and miss the connecting flight and stay here forever as an illegal, make money, dig through rubbish, eat steak, eat carrion, live in a skyscraper with a view of the Great Towers, spend the night under a bridge. However you do it, just get here. Just to become a Cityzen, if only for a while, to become a denizen of the City, in a population consisting entirely of immigrants of some generation or another (yes, I know that 5% of the population are still natives, you can see their strict hawk-like faces in the films of the Great Cinema, but you won't come across them on the streets). Everybody wants to get here. I did too. And so did Sasha.

At night I lie and think: there, at home, on the other side of the planet, on the broken cobbled square of our miserable city, artists are still selling paintings of the City. "The City by Day" – suspension bridges in a golden cocoon of sunlight; "The City by Night" – headlights and the neon skeletons of high-rises in the darkness. Naïve. They've never seen the City. But I know what the days are like here: all the bridges, all the streets and squares are crawling with Cityzens – lazy and gluttonous, like dragonfly larvae – and the enormous towers block out the sun permanently. And I know what the nights are like here too: they're brighter than the days. In the Great City you never get that calm, impenetrable darkness that the artists back home put on their canvases… There are glowing slogans everywhere, neon curses. "You don't have to live in the City. But if you do live in the City, you've got to be happy." ""You can worship any gods you choose, but only if you're wearing decent shoes."

This town doesn't advertise, it revels in itself.

...And back home the poets still write excruciating blank verse poems about the City. Back home writers send their heroes, lyrical and otherwise, out on to the streets of the Great City. Back home students study "the image of the City" in literature. Back home philosophers discuss the role of the City in history. Back home politicians and economists discuss the role of the City in the financial crisis. And not one of them has a valid visa for the City, let alone leave to remain.

I do, for now.

Young directors shoot movies about the City on film lots in Prague or Mumbai. Back home, we didn't watch these young directors' films, we watched TV shows made in the City. For the most part they were made on sound stages – talking heads, endless dialogues, over-the-shoulder shots. But we waited for the Great City to flash by in some scene. And we watched them without subtitles – learning the language, picking up City slang so we could use those same words later on social media…

On my Facebook every third post was about the City. Someone would upload photos with views of the City nicked off people who had really been there. Aging "creatives" – the sort that wear beaten up screen-print T-shirts (the City by day, the City by night) under expensive jackets – would describe their role in some ordinary everyday scenario that could hardly have taken place anywhere but the City. And they'd drop City slang from the TV shows into their conversations.

I wore those T-shirts too. And dropped that same City-slang. Now I know: people don't really talk like that here.

Back home, in my home country, every day, against a backdrop of static pictures of the city (the City by day, the City by night), female newsreaders with peroxide hair would inform us tetchily about how bad life was in the City. Industrial action, shoot-outs, hunger strikes, disasters, diseases, obesity, tornados, corrupt cops, prostitutes, feral teens. The voices of the peroxide newsreaders tremble with rage. They have been refused visas to the City; they're blacklisted. They're lying, the bitches. The Great City is wallowing in happiness. And if someone is having a bad time there, then it's got nothing to do with tornados.

They're lying – and their images are lying too. The City by day. The City by night.

At night I lie there and listen to the laughter, and the music, and the cries of pain and pleasure, the screech of tyres on tarmac, the howling, the rasping. It's the City singing me its terrifying lullaby. Proper lullabies are always terrifying. Go to sleep, go to sleep, otherwise the beast will come out of the woods. Sleep, don't cry, otherwise your mother will give you away to a witch… In all cultures the songs of night are the most frightening: if you don't go to sleep, you'll die. All the more so in the City – here they really know how to take something to extremes, to turn the volume up to the max.

But I'm a stranger here, I haven't passed a single Test, and the terrifying song of the City does not lull me to sleep. And Sasha is gone, Sasha, whose whispering could silence that song.

I lie there and count the days – how many left until the end of my life in the City. Until the end of the "cultural exchange programme" I'm on. Until the end of my lease on this shitty flat. Until the day I fly back.

I've already bought souvenirs. I thought to do this ahead of time, while there is at least still some money on my City-card. I'm going to give my mother a book on "The Art of the City". My brother – some whisky. And I'm giving Shulinsky some sneakers. Proper City-kicks, understated, the colour of cigarette ash – not that crap he goes about in back home, convinced that they're really these awesome trainers from the City.

I remember him sitting outside the café back home, his feet propped on an empty chair. On the day we picked up our passports from the consulate. Shulinsky was always trying to get his feet up a bit higher, at every convenient moment, it was like a reflex: he had the City logo on the soles of his shoes. Whenever he had to take his shoes off – for instance, round at our house – he'd casually kick his trainers off in the corridor. So casually that he'd leave them with the sole facing upwards... Bright green, the colour of an unripe tomato, so fake. You can get shoes like that here, in theory, but they're considered bad taste... He sat there, his foot propped up on an empty chair, adjusting his sock a little. He said:

"You know, you'll definitely have to do a Test when you're over there."

He said it in a nasty way, a mean way, as if he had more to say somehow. As if at the last moment he'd swallowed the end of the sentence: "...and you'll screw it up."

He was jealous. He thought he should be going instead of me. Year after year we would fill out visa applications, stand in the mile-long queue snaking outside the embassy and answer those humiliating questions ("Do you intend to work as a prostitute in the City? Do you intend to engage in begging?") in the hope of winning a City-coupon, and we'd try and think up some Project so we could get a City-grant or take part in some kind of cultural exchange programme. Year after year we would book a table in the incredibly expensive café opposite the embassy in order to get drunk after the latest failure. The latest rejection.

And then they went and gave me a visa, one which even had a "plus one", and not him. I drank in moderation, but felt drunk even so. I didn't want too much alcohol to disrupt this feeling of harmony – all those chemicals, the endorphins, the volatile organic compounds that had come together inside me to make this formula for happiness. He was knocking it back furiously and wouldn't look at me.

"So are you going to take Sasha with you?"

"Of course."

"Idiot."

I suddenly realised: he, perhaps, was hoping that the "plus one" would be him. But of course I was planning on taking Sasha. It's nice going with a mate if it's just a two-week jolly. But for six months you don't take a mate, you take a woman. To cook the food, clean the dishes, hoover, fuck etc.

"You do know that in the City..." He finally looked me in the eye. "They say that in City everyone splits up. Couples fall apart there."

"We're not going to split up," I said. "And we're not going to fall apart."

I bought Sasha a present too – in case I find her in the end. Or we meet in the airport. Or she's already home, she's gone back before me. I'm going to give her an amulet to protect from evil spirits – the opal one in the window, the one she's been looking at for ages. Sometimes at night I take it out of its blue velvet box and hold it tight in my hand. I don't know why. It doesn't save me from the insatiable spirit of the city.

...Only just before morning does the City spit me out into a dream, having eaten its fill of me.

This dream is draining and monotonous, like working as a seamstress in a factory. It's as if I'm standing at a machine and sewing, sewing together a fabric made from my dreams, which then unravels like cheap Chinese viscose. The City is making me work for it even in my sleep. Sticking dark rags together, linking them with rough stitches. A dream about plucking a bird alive stuck to a dream in which my mother is calling to me in a strange voice, stuck to a dream in which Sasha has something sharp sticking out of her tongue.

I wake up exhausted, like a worker returning from a night shift.

Later, in the day, when I go out to look for Sasha, I see hideous black and red clothes in the windows of the big shops. They look like my dreams.

I don't know where Sasha went. She didn't say anything. But there are fewer and fewer days until we leave, fewer days to find her.

Shulinsky was right. I screwed up, royally. I lost my girlfriend. And I didn't pass a single Test.

The first Test came, it seems, straight after landing. I'm not talking about passport control, but *that* Test. I hadn't expected it to happen so quickly, so I didn't even realise. Then, later, when Sasha suggested that that's what it had been, it hit me like an electric shock: but of course. On the way out of the airport, by the taxi rank, there was a cat crawling across the hot tarmac. We figured it had been hit by a car – one of these taxis must have hit it; its back legs didn't work, it dragged them along as it crawled, and its tail too; it crawled in a circle, in jerks and jolts, as if trying to escape from its own half-dead body. But there was no blood. Later I realised how strange it was that there was no blood… Sasha said that we should take it to a vet. Which was ridiculous: we've just got off the plane, we're tired and sweaty and didn't sleep last night, and here she is suggesting that instead of going to the hotel we try and save a sick, filthy cat. We have no idea what sort of germs this cat may have. And how disgusting it would be to touch it. I told her no. No vets, we're going to the hotel, that cat is going to die whatever happens.

A taxi driver pulled up. I chucked our bags in the boot and got in the car. Sasha didn't. She took off her jumper and wrapped the cat in it, inexpertly, as if she were swaddling a baby for the first time.

"Give me the address," Sasha said. "Leave the address of the hotel on a piece of paper."

"Forget the cat and get in the car."

The cat howled, loud and plaintive, exactly like a baby.

"Write down the address. I'll be along later."

I was furious. I wasn't going to write anything down for her and, as we drove away, I said:

"You know the name of the hotel."

She got in late in the evening. On her jeans there were the encrusted traces of something yellowy-brown. She went to the bathroom to wash off the stains.

"There are three hotels in this town with the same name. I nearly didn't find it."

"How's your cat doing?" I asked.

"They put her to sleep. They said I'd done the right thing bringing her in. Otherwise she'd have been in pain for a lot longer." She threw her wet jeans on the floor and undressed completely.

I sat on the bed and watched her washing herself in the shower. The wall between the bathroom and the bedroom was made of glass. The other wall – between the bedroom and the city – was glass too. I got up and drew the blinds.

"Why've you closed the blinds?" she shouted through the noise of the water. "I like the view from the window.

It was an expensive hotel, and the view really was impressive. A whole forest of City-towers growing into the asphalt.

"I don't want people to see you naked."

"They can't see from over there. And even if they can, I couldn't care less."

Now that really infuriated me. That habit of hers of wandering around the house naked and not "caring less" that some passer-by might see her.

"... Did you hear me? They said I'd done the right thing! I reckon it was a Test..."

I lay down on the bed and closed my eyes. I pictured the crippled cat. Paralysed. At the taxi rank. With no blood.

A Test. Well, of course. And I'd failed it.

"...if they said I did the right thing then that means I passed, right?" She turned off the water and, without drying off, came into the bedroom.

"Do you honestly believe that *you* are going to have a Test here?" I let out a wheezy, old-mannish sort of chuckle.

She nodded. Drips of water from her wet hair landed on me. She laughed and nodded even quicker.

I wiped my face, feeling hot rage filling the skin beneath my fingers.

"It's me who'll be doing the Tests here, Sasha. You're just a 'plus one'. So don't go getting your hopes up."

She carried on smiling, but her nipples suddenly became small and sharp, as if they were about to prick me.

Later I softened what I'd said somehow, later we made love and drank whisky; but I remember her standing in front of me, covered in goosebumps and drips, with hard nipples, with a smile, and I realise, only now, so late, only now do I realise that it was for her that the City had set up a Test, on the very first day, and that she had let this city inside her, she had given herself to it quickly and easily, she had absorbed the first drop of its venom. And on the very first day a connection had been made between her and the City. On the very first day she had cheated on me with this city. It had used dirty tricks to take her, luring her in like a child with a sick little pussy cat. To take her from me.

She took everything in her stride. The noise. The light. The crowds. The greasy food. The heat. The bites. It doesn't taste good, so what. It's itchy, so what, no big deal. She slept at night. She wasn't bothered by the poisonous light. She wasn't bothered by the music day and night. Once she'd seen how smooth the women's legs were here, she would go round the shops, searching for these magic gels. She had fine white skin and after shaving she would get little inflamed bumps on her legs. She would buy all these little multi-coloured tubes and bottles and rub them into her skin several times a day, filling the room with the smell of mint, lavender, coconut and something honeyish and sweet; there really were fewer and fewer little red bumps on her legs, but she thought they weren't going down fast enough. I told her that I didn't care, that I liked her legs the way they are, but she said: it's not like that here, people don't do that here. She wasn't interested in just being attractive to me anymore. She wanted to be attractive to the City.

She was having fun. She'd say that she felt invigorated by the City's energy. Even when we moved from the five-star hotel into a one-room hovel called a "studio", she was still happy with everything.

No one had warned us that the hotel wasn't for the entire stay. One day the concierge just left an envelope on the bedside table – a pus-green envelope, the smell and colour of money that has passed through lots of clammy, greasy hands. "Dear Guest! The official section of your cultural exchange programme in the City has come to an end. We hope that it has been interesting and informative and that in this time you have managed to write at least half of your Work dedicated to our City. We have transferred sufficient funds for the rest of your stay in the City to your City-card. We suggest that you and your +1 budget your funds carefully and rent one of the small but cosy studios listed below. We hope that this will give you a chance to feel like a Cityzen for a while and to successfully complete your Work dedicated to the City. We would like to wish you every success in your creative endeavours and to thank you for taking part in the events programme."

The last "event" had actually taken place the very day the letter came. It was called: "East European Writers in Conversation with the Readers of the City." We arrived fifteen minutes before it started. In the conference hall of the Central Library, which could accommodate a thousand people, there were six of us. Four writers (me, Sokhin the crime novelist, Artyomov the fantasy writer, and some pimply Polish essayist), an interpreter (a smartly dressed lady with a luxurious hair-do and the nervous look of an illegal immigrant awaiting deportation at any moment) and a moderator (a smooth, well-groomed fellow with fishy eyes). We went up on the stage and took up our places by the microphones. The moderator, without even looking in our direction, asked, through the interpreter, whether we were planning on reading from our books and then, immediately, without waiting for a reply, added that it would make sense if we only presented excerpts from the works about the City that we'd been writing as part of the exchange programme, because nothing else would be of any interest to a local audience. Artyomov nodded energetically and immediately started digging through his laptop looking for "the most killer bit", as he put it. The moderator slid his gaze squeamishly over the screen and nodded. Sokhin modestly refused to read, and whispered conspiratorially to me that he hadn't even started on his Work yet and that right now he'd quite fancy getting a bite to eat.

I decided to read my bit about the High Way – a motorway which the

Cityzens had transformed into an urban park symbolising the symbiosis of humankind, nature and the metropolis; it went right under the window of our hotel room. Back then I still liked this joke: the road markings, all the signs and so on, the lighting at night and the barriers have all been left, and here and there, right in the road, there are the rusting skeletons of cars, but the central reservations are planted with flowers and there are sycamores along the sides – God knows how they grow there, how they squeeze in, where they thrust their powerful roots – as well as palms, and shrubs... You can go for a walk there, or sit on a bench and drink a coffee, and beneath you is the City and above you is the City and it's like you're in the main artery leading to the heart of the Great City, and you can feel it beating. Back then it all still seemed like that, or maybe it didn't any more but I was just trying really hard to maintain a positive image of the City. Now I couldn't care less about that image, and I've got nothing to lose, so I'm letting myself write the truth. The High Way is a snake coiled threateningly above the city, covered in dead asphalt scabs. Inside it the roots of the plants are woven into a solid rotting mass. There can be no symbiosis between humankind, nature and the City. This city has devoured nature and humanity and is grinding them down without respite. The High Way is not an artery leading to its heart, but the oesophagus leading to its stomach. Or maybe its bowels...

...In the end I didn't read my positive piece about the City that day in the Central Library (later I deleted it, and lots of other fragments too). We waited ten minutes, fifteen, and then ten more – but no one came. When half an hour had passed, someone did turn up – a dowdy, sickly, cheaply dressed little woman in her fifties. The only person in the City who was interested in the writers of Eastern Europe. She didn't have a ticket, but rather a free voucher which allowed her to attend events at the library. For some reason she showed it to us, as if we were bus conductors, studied it for a long time herself, and then, constantly checking the voucher, sought out *her* row in the absolutely deserted hall and started making her way to *her* seat, squeezing her sharp elbows tight to her body, as if she were afraid of knocking into someone. At last she took her seat, folded her arms across her chest and pursed her lips truculently.

For about a minute, we looked at her, and she at us. Then, slowly and laboriously, like a trained monkey, she started clapping her hands. The claps were crisp and resonant, like dry twigs snapping.

"According to the rules of the library, we can't begin an event until there are more than three people in the audience," the moderator said flatly, examining a hangnail on his finger.

"I'll wait," responded the woman.

"If no one comes in the next ten minutes, we'll end the session," said the moderator.

"I have a voucher for this event!"

"I'm sorry. Those are the rules."

The woman nodded obediently.

"So much the better," Sokhin, the author, said loudly. "Now we can go and get something to eat."

"Let's get Chinese," Artyomov chimed in. "I think there's a Chinatown here, it should be authentic."

"Or Korean maybe… Would you care to join us?" Sokhin asked the moderator and the interpreter.

The interpreter turned away.

"I would prefer a Chinese restaurant," the Polish essayist said reedily. "On the corner here there's one where you only pay to get in and then you can eat as much as you like."

Slouching in her chair, the woman listened intently, her expression suggesting this was some literary discussion which she just couldn't quite catch the meaning of.

"Thanks to all of you who have come to our 'meet the writers' event." The moderator got up. "We look forward to seeing you at other library events." He nodded briefly then left the room. The interpreter trotted after him silently.

"Right then, Chinese? Eat as much as we like?"

"I'm not hungry," I said. "I'd just like a quick cup of coffee."

"Suit yourself." Sokhin hurried to the exit. "But we're going for some grub."

I turned to the woman. She was sitting in the same pose as before. On the top of her head there was a brush of short grey hair with rare flashes of black. She inspired feelings of both squeamishness and pity. I decided that pity should win out: "Do you fancy a coffee?"

She stood up indecisively.

"I take it this would strictly be a meeting between an author and a reader?"

I held back my laughter. This wretched, badly dressed fifty-something creature with clipper-cut hair, was, it seems, seriously worried – or seriously hoping – that I might be interested in her as a woman.

"Yes, it will be a meeting between an author and a reader," I said.

She nodded and trotted up to me warily, like a stray dog that's been lured over with a whistle and doesn't know whether it's going to get a kick or a bit of sausage.

Why did I invite her along? Just out of politeness and pity? Or did I suspect that it was a Test? The latter most likely. Here you go, a tiny orphaned little person that no one gives a toss about. But if you do give a toss, if you show her some respect, some warmth, demonstrate that you're simple, open, no attitude, no airs and graces – you just wait, they'll think highly of you too.

The writers of Eastern Europe headed off to a restaurant, and she led me down narrow, stinking back alleys to some "nice little place" she knew. She was wearing a polyester polo neck tucked into her trousers and hideous Chinese shoes. She walked quickly, but somehow crookedly, leaning to one side, with a wooden Pinocchio gait.

"Chinese, Chinese..." she muttered. "The Chinese have taken over this whole street. When I moved here, thirty-three years ago, there wasn't a single one. But they're like cockroaches, you see: all it takes is for one to come crawling over at the sniff of some food and suddenly you've got a whole swarm of them, all breeding non-stop..."

I walked along and said nothing. Maybe it's a test. All these politically incorrect outbursts. Agreeing would be a mistake.

She took me to some tiny Chinese caff, one so cheap that they wouldn't take my City-card, so I couldn't pay for the coffee. I asked if she could pay for me. I said that I'd take the money out at a cash machine as soon as we left and give it back to her. For my coffee and for hers. She cast a prickly, offended glance my way, and then spent an age digging through her oilcloth handbag, picking out coins.

"Writers are often hard up," she said as she paid. "It's my treat. You're probably hungry? Your friends didn't ask you to join them. I know that sort of person..."

"I have money on my card," I repeated. "And I really don't want to eat."

"Of course. On your card." She took a noisy slurp from the cup, holding out to one side a pale bony little finger.

The coffee was disgusting – instant. The cups were dirty, with brown stains and traces of lipstick.

"Go on, tell me all about it," she said in a businesslike way.

"About what?"

"Tell me about life outside the City. I emigrated thirty-three years ago. In that time, things must have got absolutely terrible *over there*."

"Erm, I wouldn't say so. Actually, in a lot of ways it's better; a lot has changed..."

"I didn't ask you about what's 'better'," the woman said harshly. "I'm not interested in that. I want to hear about all the unhappy people. Over there."

"So you think I should only tell you things you want to hear?" I asked warily.

"I'm paying. So yes."

Maybe this isn't a Test after all, I thought. Just a crazy, crackpot woman. Unhappy. Poor. Badly dressed. Ill too, perhaps.

"There are, in truth, unhappy people everywhere." I switched on world-weary writer mode. "Back home, and over here too..."

"Here, in the City?" she cackled, bearing her yellow rat-like teeth. "There are no unhappy people in the City. Here everybody must be happy and everybody is happy. Because everybody wants to get to the City. Not everybody manages. But I did, thirty-three years ago. I don't have a job, but I get unemployment benefit. And I'm happy. I love this city. Are you really not happy here? Tell me you like everything about the City and you don't want to go back home."

"The City is interesting," I murmured and instantly got angry with myself. And at her too. Quite some methods these. And talk about extortion – take a sip of some grim coffee and then, on command, sing little birdy, pour your heart out in praise of the City! That's not one of the requirements. The requirement is a Work dedicated to the City.

"I don't like everything about the city," I said.

She narrowed her eyes:

"What is it that you don't like?"

"Are you going to rat on me?"

Crimson blotches covered her earthy grey cheeks. I mentally congratulated myself on failing the Test.

"There is no such verb as 'to rat' in our language," she said in the language of the City, with a horrific Slavic accent. "Answer my question. What is it that you don't like?"

"I don't like your methods for one."

"What methods?"

"All these Tests. These questions. The constant state of tension you keep people in. Trying to catch them out at every step. Unfair methods."

"I don't know what you're talking about." Some drool, brown from the coffee, slipped out of her mouth and hung on her chin. "Everything in the City is fair. People are treated with respect in the city."

"Was it respect that made them ask me those questions in the application?" I said angrily.

"What questions?"

"'Do you intend to engage in prostitution or begging in the City?' I'm a famous writer, and they're asking me if I engage in prostitution! That's disrespectful if you ask me."

"And if you ask me, it's you who's disrespectful. Why are you putting yourself above everyone else? You think that they can ask an ordinary shop assistant that, but not you for some reason?"

"Not the shop assistant either..." I was at a bit of a loss. "It's not right to humiliate a shop assistant with those questions either."

"Why is it so humiliating? Do you have no respect for a poor man who has to beg for alms? Or a fallen woman who has to sell herself? Do you think they shouldn't be given City-visas?"

I suddenly noticed that this conversation was making me nauseous. It was her pushiness, her blunt aggression, the gaps in her logic. It felt as if, right here in this stuffy dump of a cafe, we were driving along a rutted, pothole-covered road, accelerating, then braking, then turning sharply.

"My friend wasn't given a City-visa," I said, apropos nothing. "He's a writer too."

"He obviously didn't deserve one then. And they shouldn't have given you one either. You come here, all expenses paid, and you badmouth this Great City of ours, which is funding your trip, and you treat people with no respect. I don't like you. The City's too good for you."

"Is that the report you're going to give on me?"

She got up, saying nothing, and headed to the exit with that broken doll walk of hers.

"Wait, I have to pay you back!"

She turned round. She stuck out a long, grey-tinged tongue and licked her lips.

"It was my treat."

I jumped up and ran to the toilet. I vomited coffee and bile.

When I came back, the woman had already gone. The Chinese woman pointed irritatedly at the door – either she was explaining where she had gone, or she wanted to me to get the hell out of there.

...That same evening the letter came about our eviction from the hotel. "The official section of your cultural exchange in the City has come to an end." But of course. She went and did it. Any idiot could tell that this "reader" had informed on me to the relevant authorities.

"I think you're paranoid," Sasha said. "That doesn't sound like a Test. Just a run-of-the-mill street crazy, there's tons of them here."

"You weren't there."

"But you told me all about it."

"And this?" I shook the letter under her nose. "You think this is completely unrelated, do you?"

She looked at me pretending not to understand.

"Completely unrelated. It's just a notification about moving. We need to get our things together so we're ready to go in the morning."

We packed our bags, then I vomited again and refused to go for dinner. Sasha offered to stay with me, but I said there was no need. It's not so bad that I can't just sit here on my own. She twirled in front of the mirror, tried on different outfits, put on mascara and smeared oily potions on her insufficiently smooth legs. She said that she was going to the café on the corner, but I knew that she was heading for the bar on the nineteenth floor, which in the evenings was packed with fashionable young people.

"Are you sure you're OK?" she asked from the doorway.

"Yes. Off you go."

And she went.

I was furious. Asking whether I'm OK. So thoughtless, so hypocritical. And to then just up and go, leaving me in the middle of all these open-mouthed suitcases. When it's clear that I'm not OK at all, that I'm in a bad way, that I'm being turned inside out.

I shouldn't have drunk that disgusting coffee. I shouldn't have been living off fast food every day – all this City street-food, so wonderfully aromatic, so tasty, so tender – while it's still warm. But the more it cools, the more inedible it becomes. It's like you're chewing something artificial, a plasticine replica… I suddenly realised that the last time I ate was the day before. I've got to have something to eat. Real, good, hot food, that's what I need, a hot lump of meat. I didn't have the strength to leave the hotel, and ordered room service. A chop with some rice. The night porter rolled in a steaming plate under a lid on a silvery trolley, and I paid with my City-card, some unbelievable amount. I devoured it, choking it down, swallowing big unchewed chunks, while it's hot, the most important thing is to eat it all up while it's hot. Then I lay down under the duvet, in my clothes, and curled up into a ball. I imagined the hot meat cooling inside me, turning into cold, tough rubber. I heaved again. Dry, barren spasms. Something solid had attached itself to my insides and didn't want to come out.

Sasha came back in the middle of the night, drunk and with lipstick smeared around her mouth. I pretended to be asleep. She kissed me on the forehead, like a child. She smelled of whisky and, for some reason, strawberries.

The "studio" turned out to be a stinking little room with a hot plate, a fridge and a shower room. At night translucent gnats would crawl through the torn mosquito net. When they had sucked their fill of blood, they would turn a dark crimson colour. I would whack them with a newspaper and they would burst like poisonous berries. It left shapeless brown marks on the wall.

"Don't kill them," Sasha whispered. "New ones will just come anyway."

I was sleeping terribly, I felt terrible, I was itching all over, we didn't make love any more. Sasha would kiss my bites and purr in my ear: "Don't worry, it'll pass... Hang on in there, it'll all be over soon, it won't last forever..." Her whispering would make things slightly better and I would fall asleep.

I barely ate. I went round all the nearby pharmacies looking for stomach medication – without success. The pharmacies in the City are for healthy people. Huge rooms piled high with creams, perfumes, deodorants, condoms, fans, dildos, tissues, towels, combs, toners, shaving sets, essential oils and vitamins.

"Can I help you, sir?" they would say to me, the sales girls with the long smooth legs that Sasha dreamed of.

"I need medicine."

"Medicine?"

"Yes, medicine."

The smiles slipped from their faces.

"What, are you ill?"

"I need the medicines section."

They would lead me all the way through the shop, trying to keep their distance, and then further along cluttered corridors into a basement room which smelled of old men and mould and where there really were some little bottles and boxes on shelves, and then they would quickly make themselves scarce. I'd wait an age before someone would come out to see me. As a rule, no one would even come, and I would make my way back out. Sometimes some fat old black woman would appear, give me a frosty, suspicious looking over, listen to my request and demand to see a prescription from a doctor. I didn't have a prescription – my medical insurance only covered physical injuries and heart attacks, and I didn't have enough money on my City-card for an appointment – and the black woman would grumpily tell me to have a nice day.

"I've found you a doctor that's not too expensive," Sasha said.

"Where did you find them?"

"Some friends of mine gave me the address."

Friends. That stung. She has "friends" here.

"Male?"

"What?"

"Male friends?"

She looked at me in a strange, slightly pitying sort of way. Like a laboratory frog after a leg has been amputated. It scared me. I asked her:

"Sasha, is there someone else?"

Another pitying look.

"It doesn't work like that here," she said.

"What doesn't work like that?"

"Here… how should I put it? There's always someone else. Male or female. And everybody takes whoever they want."

"And do you take them too? And do you get taken, you slut?" I was shuddering heavily. As if there was someone inside me, someone alien, someone crazy, biting painfully, trying to gnaw his way out so he could charge at her and kill her. Bite her slender neck.

I lit a cigarette. It went out. I sparked it up again. Bloody tobacco in this city. Burns so badly. It's not proper tobacco.

She watched my hand shaking as I smoked.

"No, I don't take anyone," she said, sounding like a schoolgirl. "And I'm not taken either. I am not a slut. All I've done is find you a reasonably priced doctor."

I kissed her hands and begged forgiveness and she nodded patiently. I lit another cigarette and offered her one, but she said she'd quit. I took a drag – the cigarette went out.

"You were right to quit. There's no proper tobacco here anyway."

She frowned uncomprehendingly:

"The tobacco's fine. It's just bad for you. You should quit too."

"The reasonably priced doctor" turned out to be an old woman, one of the natives, with a hook nose and dark, wrinkled skin like a sun-dried date. The appointment was in a tiny little room hung with amulets and rattling trinkets and smelling of scented candles. She felt my belly with her clawed fingers, nestled her ear against my chest and looked into my eyes. Her eyes were like olives rotting in oil – bluey-black, clouded and weepy.

"There's a demon living inside him," she told Sasha in the language of the City. "An evil spirit. It is devouring your man. I can drive out the evil spirit."

I burst out laughing. But Sasha didn't laugh, and there was fear in her eyes.

"I will drive out the evil spirit – for money." The old woman pinched her fingers together and rubbed her thumb against her index and middle fingers, then said it again: "Money."

"Let's get out of here," I said to Sasha. "It's a con."

"Maybe we should pay her?" she looked doubtfully at the old woman. And at me the same way.

"No. We're leaving," I dragged her out after me.

"That's the demon speaking for him," the old woman cawed after us.

Strange as it may seem, after that trip to "the doctor" I started feeling much better. It was probably all psychosomatic. I dealt with it by force of will alone – just to prove to Sasha that there were no demons inside me. But I was still tired and irritable, probably from lack of sleep. I was spending whole days on the Work; she tried to help. Do you fancy something to eat, go on I'll run and get something, I'll get some pizza, what do you want on yours? I snarled: bring me whatever, can't you see I'm busy? She brought me something. This is disgusting. She went out to get another one. I feel so bad, oh God, I feel so bad about the way I treated her. She was like a guardian angel and I drove her away. One time I made her go and get something like five different pizzas in one evening. The final one she brought was vegetarian, with mushrooms.

"Don't you know I hate mushrooms?"

She said:

"If you don't want the mushrooms, don't eat them."

"Then pick them off my slices."

She said:

"I'm not your servant."

I should have stopped. At that moment I ought to have shut up; I even wanted to, but for some reason it didn't work, and I spoke, I spoke in a strange, hoarse voice:

"You're a slut. You're a parasite. You're a plus one. I'm paying for your life here. I'm paying for you to go off whoring. You're a nobody. Without me you'd never have got to the City."

She smiled – a cold, empty smile that scared me.

She said:

"These things are decided by the City. I would have got here anyhow, with or without you."

She said:

"The City is my city. I love the City."

She said:

"I feel like a Cityzen."

She said:

"I am happy in the City."

She talked like that woman, the reader at the Central Library. She was like a doll, with this City-patriotism of hers, like a long-legged, busty doll.

She said:

"I've read the thing you're writing about the City. Your Work. It's terrible."

She said:

"There's so much hate in it. So much darkness, so much filth."

She said:

"The City is a city of love, and you've dragged it through the mud."

She talked and I looked at how smooth her legs had become. And tanned. Perfect legs.

That same evening she left. Without her things, without any money, without a City-card. She didn't say where she was going. She kissed me goodbye on the forehead. Couples split up. I'd been warned. I should have run after, kissed her smooth legs, stopped her, begged her. I should have looked after her. Not let her go out into this lecherous, insatiable, rumbling, grumbling city. But I said to her:

"Get out."

I knew that couples split up.

Fatty Man is sitting, as usual, by the entrance to the underground on his torn up cardboard box, collecting change from passers-by. He's not fat at all, quite the opposite, he's hungry and skinny, he just really likes talking about how he was once this terrible fatty: "You know what, man, time was I lived in the best hotels in the City and I'd be stuffing my face from morning to night and I was this huge fatty, like this, man!" No one knows – and no one cares – what he was like before. But everyone calls him Fatty and Man, because he loves those words.

When he sees me, Fatty Man starts wriggling busily and smacking his lips. Fatty Man is used to getting a coin or a bit of food from me, that's been the way since our first day in the studio. Sasha thought that we should definitely give him some change. Beggars are given special treatment in the City, how you react to them could be part of a Test. Fatty Man stretches an upturned palm out towards me, but I don't have anything on me today. I'm tired, I don't know where to start looking for Sasha and I haven't got much money left to last me the three days until I leave.

"Sorry, Fatty," I say and walk on past.

He whimpers indignantly.

"Hey, man! In this town we treat beggars with a little respect."

I keep walking.

"I heard you're trying to find your woman?" he shouts at my back.

I stop. I go back to him.

"Do you know where Sasha is?"

"Everybody knows where your little bit of skirt is. Nice little bit. Everybody knows her."

"Where is she?" I take him by the shoulders and shake him. His clothes stink, and are somehow greasy to the touch. Fatty grins:

"You're looking in the wrong place. You should look for her in the Red District. With the whores."

I punch him in the face and something crunches under my fingers. He screeches briefly, and then draws it out, loud and plaintive, like a banshee:

"He hit me! He hit a beggar, ow, he hit me, hit me..!"

He yells, and everyone turns to look at us and blood and snot flow from his nose and drip on the cardboard. A police car drives past us, and I wait for them to grab me and put me in an armlock, but they drive past, not caring.

"You're done for now," whines Fatty Man. "That's the last you'll see of the City. You have no idea who you just hit, man! There's more to me than meets the eye, more than meets the eye, the spirit of the city is in me, and I have tested you!"

"I don't give a shit about your tests!" I roar in reply, and everyone turns round to look at us again.

Fatty gets up and, staggering and dripping blood, heads into the underground.

A day before I'm due to leave the City I reread the finished Work. It's terrible, that's what she said. And what do you know, she's right. There's so much hate in it. So much darkness, so much filth. The Great City dragged through the mud... I don't care. Let them read it and get a nasty shock when they see what a God-forsaken place they live in. They can put a stamp in my passport blacklisting me forever. I'm not planning on coming back here anyway. I send the Work to the City Cultural Exchange Committee.

The evening before we are due to leave the City I end up going to the Red District. Our flight is tomorrow, and I have to be certain that Sasha's not here.

Or that she is here. I promise myself that I won't offend her, insult her, shout at her – I'll just take her by the hand and lead her away. And tomorrow we'll fly home.

The prostitutes – women, men, transsexuals – look at me with indifference; I obviously don't look like a potential client. I show them a photograph of Sasha. No one here knows who she is.

For many hours I wander around the district, to no avail. I'm both happy and dead with grief: she's not here. Fatty Man lied. She's not here. My Sasha isn't here.

I'm already hailing a taxi when some girl calls me over.

"Hold up, mate! I know her. In the photo. You wanna pick her up, right?"

I force my frozen lips to move.

"Yes. I want to. To pick her up."

The girl gestures for me to follow here. She has a limp, but moves quickly enough. We go into a shop called Adult Toys, cross the shop floor and go downstairs into a smoky basement room

"Wait here," she says in a whisper and hides behind a curtain.

I prepare myself to see Sasha – in a leather skirt and a gold scaly top, her face puffy and covered in make-up, her legs smooth and tanned – but that same girl comes back into to the room alone. She's naked. From the knee down her right leg is a wooden prosthetic.

"Where's Sasha?"

She laughs.

"I don't know any Sasha. What do you need that slut for? Come here, I'll give it to you absolutely free of charge…"

She totters towards me, stretching her arms out:

"I'll do you for free… Touch me, feel how wet I am, I haven't had sex in three years!"

I push her away, and she falls, the prosthetic clattering. It falls off and rolls along the floor, right at me.

I run between the shelves of dildos and strawberry-scented vibrators, I run down the streets, pushing past the whores and their drunken clients, I run and I keep hearing this rumbling noise. A wooden leg rolling over a wooden floor.

I leave the key to the studio on the table, take the bags – my things and Sasha's – and slam that door forever. She'll be there, I say to myself. She'll come to the airport. She won't miss our flight.

The airport is like a smashed up ants' nest in a mouldering tree stump, everyone is dashing about, running apart and clashing together, with all their possessions, and I try in vain to spot Sasha.

"My plus one," I say to the girl at check-in when I give her the bags. "I had a plus one with me on the trip."

"And?" the girl raises a drawn-on thread of an eyebrow in irritation.

"I want to know whether she's gone through check-in yet."

"I cannot divulge information of that kind."

"But she's my wife!"

"I'm sorry but those are our rules."

At passport control a black man, gloomy and paunchy like a thunder cloud, studies my documents. Several times he checks me against my photograph. He clicks his mouse and examines something on his monitor for a long time. Finally, his face brightens:

"Congratulations! You're staying."

"What do you mean I'm staying?"

"It's very simple. The name has just come through of the winner of the competition for literary works about the City. It's you!" He bares his white teeth. "So now I'm just going to cancel your ticket… there you go! Have a nice day."

"But I didn't pass a single Test," I mumble. "There's been some kind of misunderstanding… Check your database…"

"Test?" he grins even wider. "What tests would they be?"

"I have to leave!" I try to squeeze past him. He stops smiling and blocks my way through. He places a heavy black hand on my shoulder.

"Let me through," I whine like a child. "I don't want to stay in the City. I want to go home."

"That ticket was paid for by the City. If you don't want to be a Cityzen, you'll have to pay for your own return flight. Those are our rules."

"I don't have any money," I tell him. "On my City-card. Or any cash either."

He narrows his eyes conspiratorially and slaps me on the shoulder:

"OK, man. I can see you've got the spirit of the City in you. Go on, here you go," he proffers me a couple of coins. "Go and buy yourself a drink."

My name is Writer Man. My spot is by the entrance to the metro, on the cardboard boxes. A good spot. Always lots of people. They give me change and plastic bags of leftovers. In return I tell them the story of how I was a writer in the City and how I won a competition. I say:

"You know what, man, I was such an idiot that I was planning on saving up money for a ticket to fly home from the Great City. But then I smartened up and sussed it out: everybody wants to get to the City, but not everybody does. And seeing as I've been lucky enough to have got to the City, man, I guess I'll stay here and be happy."

I also tell them that I once had a woman, a beautiful woman – I've forgotten her name:

"She left, you see man, and I went round looking for her like a total idiot.

Then I sussed it out: what do I need that woman for when the cripple girl in the Red District will do me absolutely free of charge?

I hold out my hand, palm up, and I'm given a coin. I say:

"Go on, man, give me another. I've got the spirit of the City in me."

## THE SEEING-EYE

"We were intrigued by your pitch. We'd like to meet ASAP and discuss everything."

"That's great. But, sorry, you are again…?"

"The creative producer."

He was calling from the metro, or maybe from some room underground – I could barely hear him. I pressed the phone to my ear as hard as I could – I was hoping he might repeat the name of the film company, or at least his own name, but he went silent. In the receiver something was scrabbling about clumsily, buzzing and crackling – it was as if a big electric beetle had caught fire in there. Flipped over on its back, its legs twitching… The name of the company was something obscure, a couple of words in English with a cosmic feel… Star Trek...? Stardust Pictures…? Star Media Group…? The line was terrible. I think I might even have caught his name but then I forgot it instantly. When I'm nervous I sometimes have problems concentrating. My ear was hot and damp, as if I'd been holding it against a boiler. I let out a deep sigh, unstuck the mobile from my ear and said:

"OK, thanks for your interest. I'd be happy to meet and discuss it. Unfortunately, I'm all booked up today and tomorrow." I forced myself to pause to try to make it sound impressive.

It's all very simple, I've already learned how to role-play these games – it's a question of status. Of who needs who more. So this is the producer calling me, the talented screenwriter – him calling me, not the other way round – with a proposal. The talented screenwriter lets the producer know that he's willing to work together, but does he have to come running at the first whistle? The screenwriter is a busy man, a man much in demand. He has a packed schedule. He has negotiations, projects…

The beetle was frying away slowly in the receiver. The creative producer still said nothing. My hope was that, while I kept this pause going, he'd suggest meeting the day after tomorrow, or at the weekend, or he'd simply ask what day would suit me… He didn't. The pause dragged on.

To make my silence sound more plausible I started leafing loudly through a notebook, gripping the mobile between my shoulder and my ear.

"It looks like I've got a slot on Friday," I bleated.

He said nothing. "Yeah, actually, pretty much the whole day… I mean it's all pretty flexible, so I could make Friday work…

"I don't want to meet on Friday," he said. The electronic beetle at his end of the line had finally died, and his "don't want to" sounded clear and crisp in the ensuing silence.

"How about the weekend then?" I even narrowed my eyes, so imploring did I sound. The phone, hot and damp, was stuck to my ear again. "Or, you know what? I'm just having a look now and I see that tomorrow evening… mmhmm, in the evening I think I might have a little bit of time."

"I heard you," the creative producer said and fell silent again.

"So it looks like tomorrow evening might suit? I'll be in town from five, so it wouldn't be a problem…"

"One in the morning," said the creative producer.

"I'm sorry?"

"Tonight, at one in the morning, come to my house. I'll text you the address."

"I brought you a little something." I held out a strawberry tart from a fancy supermarket. I had spent a long time wondering what to buy: a bottle of whisky or something sweet? Finally, I'd settled on something sweet – because, you never know, some people don't drink. What's more, the producer might consider me bringing a bottle to be a bit over-familiar. But a little something sweet – you can't go wrong with that.

He pulled it from the bag and examined the transparent plastic box; his face exuded such boredom that it was as if the box contained not a tart, but a batch of old A+ essays I'd done at school. I regretted not bringing whisky.

"Sergei." I extended my hand cheerfully, hoping that he'd also introduce himself. He touched my moist palm in silence and then immediately pulled his hand away. He had an expression on his face as if he'd just thrust his hand into the strawberry tart.

Coffee-coloured mud flowed off my shoes and onto his blonde wood floor. I scurried to take the shoes off, put them on a little shelf and then stepped my stockinged foot into the brown puddle.

"We don't have any slippers for you," the creative producer said.

"Not to worry, I'm all right..."

"There's underfloor heating."

His voice sounded thick and low – lower than on the phone – and somehow it didn't fit his short, round-shouldered body. He looked ill, or maybe just hung over: puffy eyelids, grey skin with prominent pores, murky button eyes. An ageless face – anywhere between thirty-five and fifty – a brush of short black hair, a bald patch on the crown.

"Into the kitchen," he intoned in a deep voice, looking somewhere under my feet. I automatically lowered my head to see if there was, say, some little dog I hadn't noticed that he was talking to. He turned and, shuffling in his fluffy slippers, wandered down the long corridor. There was no dog. He was talking to me.

It turned out to be a huge flat – as we walked along I counted twelve doors, several of them ajar; I saw flashes of dark, blandly furnished rooms, as if in a luxury hotel.

The space that he called the kitchen was the size of a ballroom. One entire wall was taken up by a window, with a view of the river embankment. By the window, at a cluttered round table, a man was sleeping, his head resting on the transparent table top. Outside the window, pus-yellow lumps of ice glistened beneath the streetlights in the unctuous black water. The gnawed remnant of the moon, hanging opposite the window, was exactly the same colour as the ice. You wanted to take it out of the sky and throw it where it belonged, in the river.

"Nice view," I said in a whisper. The creative producer looked at the river as if he were car sick on a bus and it was flashing by the window, then put my strawberry tart down on the table. The man woke up and took his head off the table. He had glossy flaxen curls and a huge belly.

"This is George," the creative director said. "The project director. This is Sergei."

George screwed up his face, making the shape of a smile. "What project?" I wanted to ask, but I said nothing, not wanting to alarm the embryo of hope nestling just below my heart – what if they're talking about *my* project?

"Is this the one we were talking about yesterday…?" George asked; he had a breathy, girlish voice. "Shall I give him a drink?"

The creative producer nodded. There were six or seven bottles of spirits on the table. George's puffy fingers wrapped around the neck of a bottle of Yamazaki:

"Japanese whisky. Top quality."

I quietly rejoiced that I hadn't brought some Jameson. On this table it would have looked pretty crappy – even worse than the strawberry tart.

"Give him some of the infusion instead, the one with the snake," the producer said and put a grubby round-bottomed wine glass down in front of me.

"Excellent choice." George eyed me approvingly, as if it had been my choice, put the whisky back on the table and picked up a bottle with a whitish worm curled up on the bottom. He poured each of us a glass of murky booze.

I took a sip. It was sweetish, with a metallic aftertaste.

"We like your pitch," George said coquettishly.

"Which one exactly?" I asked.

The question sounded a bit harsh and it clearly upset George, the director.

"The thing is, I've got several projects on the go at the moment," I said as tenderly as possible. The word "project" came out particularly gentle. An important word. With people like this you should use it a lot if you want to be taken seriously.

"We like all your projects," George said generously.

"Especially your latest," the creative producer specified. "I think it's called 'Inhuman'."

"'In Humans,'" I corrected him automatically, pausing after the 'In'. "Two words. But did I actually send you that one?"

I had cooked up a lot of screenplay pitches recently, seven or eight of them. Some were dear to my heart, others were written with an eye to the hypothetical "demands of the market", but most were done for very specific commissions. These commissions would, by the way, always be cancelled or politely postponed at the last minute, and I would send the pitches around to other producers along with the projects I really wanted to do and the "demands of the market" ones.

'In Humans' happened to be closest to my heart. My strongest, most interesting idea for a TV series. I'd had the idea literally days before, and I'd written it up as a pitch straight away – but I hadn't yet sent it to anyone. Or maybe I had after all? Someone at TNT maybe? When I'm nervous, I can't remember a thing.

"And what…" I wanted to confirm the name of their company or channel, but decided that would make me look like a chancer: I'd dashed off to the meeting at the first sign of enthusiasm, not even knowing who I was going to see. I buried myself in the drink, intermittently trying to choose a roundabout way of formulating the question. The brownish liquid gave my tongue and throat a pleasant pinch.

"How did you come by my pitches?"

"... We're very well connected." The creative producer took a hearty swig of the 'snakebite'. "We get sent everything on this theme."

"Theme? So it's the theme of 'In Humans' that works for you?"

" 'In Humans' doesn't work for us at all." The producer didn't even try to pretend to care. "The story is weak, the characters one-dimensional, and the idea is, let's be honest, hardly new. Basically, it's not right for us."

The embryo of hope transformed meekly into a dead worm – one just like the snake at the bottom of their brown booze. I suddenly sensed, almost physically, that this motionless worm was decomposing down there in the depths of my soul, along with the other hopes that had died in the early stages. My mouth went dry and tasted foul. I swallowed everything that was left in the glass, but that didn't help. The Vietnamese 'snakebite' had a tinge of the mortuary about it. George poured me some more.

The idea's hardly new they say! Then what the hell did they invite me here for then? Why did they call, why did we agree a time? I know why. First they'll humiliate me, then sit for a bit talking shit, and then brainstorm some ideas, feeding off my energy. Producers always feed off the energy of screenwriters, it's normal. It's not the first time this has happened to me.

All those pitches, synopses, episode breakdowns. Plot twists, multilayered characters, carefully thought-through mises-en-scène. All these storylines that are urgently, urgently required, that have already got a budget attached, that you're the only author we want for – in the end all my stories end up on the scrap heap. They're pointless. Or if they do have some point, it's not here. Perhaps they're being used by some demiurge as he creates a parallel world. Out of all of my synopses even the dumbest, most incapable deity could create a couple of pretty decent universes.

"I'm afraid I can't agree with you," I said with pride. "'In Humans' has got a strong story."

"I heard you," the creative producer said.

"There's no story there at all!" George waved a fat paw. "There's nothing to even discuss."

"But you said you liked the pitch!" I whined like a kid at nursery.

"What we like is the overall feeling," George said encouragingly.

"Strangers wearing familiar masks. Alien creatures in human skin. But what's really important is that they're not all that bad. Even from that undercooked pitch of yours it's clear – they're not monsters. They have their own truth... What is truth, brother...? It's 'District Nine' meets 'Ocean's Eleven.'" George started cawing like a crow in an imitation of laughter. "That's what we like. The fact there's nothing evil about these inhuman creatures. They are part of that power which... whatchamacallit ... They're very..." George froze.

"...Very ambiguous, very complex," I interjected.

"That's exactly it," the creative producer said didactically. "Now we're heading in the right direction."

"It's the train of thought, Sergei!" George said enthusiastically. "It's your train of thought – that's what really gives us hope!"

"You saw he brought a strawberry tart?" the creative producer said for some reason.

George's face suddenly darkened a little.

"Do you like strawberries?"

"Well... you know..." I swallowed some more 'snakebite'. "Sometimes. So you're interested in 'In Humans' after all?"

"We don't eat strawberries," said George. "Do we, brother?"

"No," the creative producer confirmed, smacking his lips strangely and reaching his hand up towards his mouth.

"What, again?" George asked: his voice sounded caring and therefore somehow girly.

The creative producer let out a moan and pulled a tooth out of his mouth.

"We're not going to discuss 'In Humans' now," he said, irritatedly turning the tooth over in his fingers — an incisor by the looks of it. "Because right now we're going to discuss another project. *Our* project. You are very suitable for it — ideologically. We're going to brainstorm."

I felt a spasm of nausea coming and took a deep breath. Maybe it's not a tooth, but a bit of food that got stuck in there? Of course it's not a tooth. You don't yank teeth out of your mouth just like that. Eat, that's what I need to do. I haven't eaten enough today. And I've drunk too much of this crap.

"Basically the story goes like this:" — the creative tossed his tooth into an ashtray — "There's been an apocalypse on earth. An epidemic caused by a terrible virus."

"Or bacteria," said George.

"This virus, or these bacteria, turns people into mutants."

"Into *hideous* mutants!" said George, deliberately emphasising the word 'hideous'.

...And these people called my idea derivative. I giggled weakly — politely, so that the sound might be taken for a sign of interest.

"Whatever you say, brother," nodded the creative producer. "Although personally I wouldn't use such a harsh word, one that's so obviously... obvious... vious... vious..." — his 's' came out with a lisp; the producer frowned — "disparaging."

The 's' in 'disparaging' had an even more pronounced lisp, as if he were saying the word 'teeth'. Looking concerned, the producer poked a finger into his mouth and started feeling the tooth.

"Is the front one wobbly?" George asked caringly. "Don't worry, it'll all be over soon. And as for 'hideous' creatures..." He turned to me. "You see, we're going to trick the viewer a bit. We're going to create this impression that the mutants are dangerous and hideous — and then, boom! — we're going to flip the viewers' assumptions upside down. It's going to blow their minds."

"We're not shaping this project to fit with what the viewer wants, what they expect," the producer chimed in animatedly. "We're creating a whole new viewer of our own. A viewer capable of sharing our vision. The sort of viewer that'll make the *medians* and *modals* look like complete rubbish! But the metamorphs — they have their own beauty, their own vuln..." — his eyes goggled — "vulnerability... khh! khh!!"

Bending his feeble body double, the producer started coughing.

"Do you need a slap on the back? Are you choking?" Not waiting for an answer, George hit him on the back.

With a quiet 'ting' one of the producer's front teeth fell onto the heated floor.

That's impossible. That sort of thing just doesn't happen. Got to eat, got to eat... I scanned the table. There was nothing there except, of course, my own offering.

"Thanks, brother," the producer nodded politely to George. "I was saying that our task is to create our own viewer. We're being very rigorous about it. We check every scene, every character, with a focus group...

He leaned over and picked his tooth up off the floor.

The floor was warm. Too warm. It was burning the soles of my feet. It was as if I was steaming them in a footbath. As if I was suffocating in steam...

"It's just a panic attack," I told myself. "I just need some air. Heart palpitations. Phantom fears. It happens to me sometimes. Doesn't it? It does. What helps is... what helps...? A distraction. If you had something to munch on..."

"And so there's this group of people trying to save the planet from the virus. And what do they do?"

"Yes, what do they do?"

The creative producer and George the director stared at me waiting for an answer.

"They try to create an antivirus," I replied mechanically and very loudly: I thought I had to push my vocal cords extra hard for my voice to break through the cloud of wooziness enshrouding me.

My answer obviously disappointed them. George half-shut his eyes and gave out a thin whining noise. The creative producer clacked something in his jaws. George started gurgling quietly, as if he were rinsing his mouth.

"But warmth and humidity help the metamorphs complete their cycle! It's a favourable microclimate for them!" said the producer heatedly, evidently continuing some argument that I'd missed the beginning of.

"But it's harmful to the outliers!" George shook his golden curls.

"Brilliant. That can be the grounds for the next conflict. Half the group wants to stay in the warm. The other half tries to shut down the thermoslots and reduce…"

"Bit of tart anyone?" I interrupted. "Do you have a knife? I'll cut it some slices."

"We don't eat strawberry tart," the creative producer said. "We don't take vitamins."

"We don't keep knives in the house."

I took the clear plastic dome off the tart, and, to my own amazement, started digging the strawberries out with my fingers and popping them in my mouth.

For a couple of seconds they observed me in silence.

"You said he was a carrier." George batted his golden eyelashes irritably.

"You never know really, brother. Not until you meet in person, not until you talk to them. But all his projects were latent. Every last one! So perhaps he'll switch. Do you remember the last seeing-eye. At first he didn't come… "

"OK, we'll give him another chance. But those strawberries… It makes you sick just to look at it."

I was devouring the strawberries, unable to stop. They were delicious and fragrant. They smelled of the forest, of pinecones, moss and putrid marshes.

"We're counting on your participation in this project, Sergei," George the director said. "You're a talented guy. An experienced guy."

They were slippery and cool, sweet and sour… I couldn't tear myself away from the strawberries and bring myself to look at him — but his voice sounded cosy and affectionate, like a grandmother praising a visiting grandson and plying him with homemade treats.

"The most important thing about our project is the twist at the end of the first series," the creative said. "The thing that everyone thought was a catastrophic epidemic turns out to be more like a vaccination. We're calling it the Primary Metamorphosis. And the real catastrophe is still to come. So now George and I are just sketching the arc of the series and you can flesh it all out later. The way we see it. You'll be the interpreter. You'll turn our vision into a screenplay. Take, for instance, the way we see the Initial Infection...

The strawberries had run out – so I could, finally, raise my head and look at the producer. Sticking out his tongue in concentration, he was eagerly scrawling something on a piece of paper. George nodded and pursed his lips into a little tube.

"Is that a Japanese character?" I asked.

"No," George said grumpily.

"Chinese?"

"We are looking for an interpreter." The producer thrust a piece of paper with the character on it right up to my face. "Do you see what I mean? We're looking for a guide, a seeing-eye. The viewer can be blind — but the screenwriter must see. So?"

I looked at the sign. It had no meaning, either explicit or symbolic. Just a collection of dots and curved lines of various lengths. But there was something about the way they combined, the way they wove around and crossed over one another, the way the fat black dots clung to the slender whiskers of the lines, that produced a sinister impression. Not outright hostility, but some kind of alien, insect logic.

It suddenly struck me that it was very important for me to turn away from this symbol and never look at it again. I wanted more strawberries. I wanted more strawberries so badly. I lowered my eyes to avoid seeing the piece of paper and started digging through the tart, pulling out the moist crumbs that were soaked through with red juice and then rolling them into balls so they'd look like berries. I made the balls, laid them out on the glass table and when there were about seven of them I gathered them all into one handful and devoured them.

"Do you think he could be the Seeing-Eye?" George said doubtfully.

"Not likely. Look at how his immune system is fighting it... It wants vitamins... It's good money," the producer suddenly spoke loudly, as if he was talking to a deaf person, and pulled the tart away from me sharply. "You'll have no complaints when it comes to money, Sergei. We've got funding. But it's not just a question of money, we all know that, right? Above all you've got to be interested in the project. It's got to get you going. Do you like Metamorphs, brother? You don't mind if I call you that, do you? You are our brother, aren't you?"

I was already chewing down the final handful of little balls, and he was still talking all the time, when I noticed it, in my peripheral vision: something's wrong. Something not right has appeared in the kitchen. Something has disappeared, and something not right has appeared in its place. Squinting, I licked my fingers for a long time, putting off the moment when I'd have to look up.

Then, from the place where the creative producer was sitting, there came an unbearable metallic screech – like a knife on a plate – and I took a look.

The producer was gone.

A big, shimmering silver sphere covered in spikes was spinning awkwardly, jerkily. Every time it turned on its axis, it would hit the glass table top with a long slender spike and make that noise. Occasionally it would freeze motionless in the air and open its needled jaw with a painful clanking noise. The needles in its jaws grew in three rows of crooked bundles.

The sphere where George the director had been sitting was spongy, porous and sticky. Not, of course, that I touched it, but I could see a mother-of-pearl slime oozing out. It was not spinning like the other sphere, but slowly contracting, pulsating softly and rhythmically. Somehow it was clear to me that this sphere was a female, and that the one with spikes was a male.

There was no fear. I didn't see any threat in their positioning. They hung quietly above me – one spinning, the other pulsating – and were obviously not planning to go on the attack. Behind them, out of the wall-sized window, I could see the watery-purple night sky over the city, and the ice moon that I wanted to pull down and chuck in the river, and the occasional lights of the houses on the far bank.

In a few gulps I knocked back the Vietnamese infusion – right out of the bottle. I don't know what came over me. There was no fear – it was something else entirely. I just decided all of a sudden that these creatures should not continue to live. Not, at least, alongside this river and this moon. And that I had to rescue mankind from them.

Carefully grabbing the bottle by the neck, I smashed it against the table so I could use it as a weapon. The blow shattered the table top (I wasn't actually planning on breaking it – I'd just forgotten it was made of glass). The snake's tiny corpse slid down my body and plopped down into the pile of shards. I raised the bottle in my hand, intending to stab the pulsating female sphere, but the spiky one was too quick for me. Buzzing and crackling threateningly, it sped towards me brandishing its long spike and jabbed me right in the solar plexus. The spike went all the way through. The bottle fell. The female sphere gave a piercing girlish squeal – and everything went dark.

"You've got a temper, brother," the creative producer said. "You've made a complete mess of my kitchen. And frightened poor old Georgie. Georgie'll be afraid of coming near you now."

I had come to in a hard chair, my arms on the armrests, in a large room with shutters drawn tight over the window. To the left and right of me there were other chairs lined up in a row. Red, like in a cinema. I didn't remember them carrying me in here, sitting me down or putting my arms on the armrests. I put my hand under my shirt and felt my stomach. There was no wound. Just smooth, hairy skin.

"I thought the spike went right through," I murmured.

"Spi-i-ke?" the creative producer drawled with mocking surprise. "What spike would that be?"

"The spheres, in the kitchen. Big spheres, they were alive, I saw them. Your sphere had spikes. I saw it."

"I hear you," the producer grinned, showing an incomplete set of teeth. "You saw big spheres and they were alive. My spheres, of course, had spikes on them."

He was mocking me. Mocking me, pure and simple.

"It was the 'snakebite', wasn't it?" For a second, I thought I understood everything. "They were just hallucinations?" For a second, the world became simple and accessible again, like a pitch for a TV show. "You put something in my drink." I tried to stand up, but couldn't.

It was as if my spine had been removed from my body. As if my body had become as soft as jelly and was slumping all over the chair.

"What did you put in my drink? What. Did. You. Put. In. It?!"

"God, how boring," the creative producer said. "A paranoid reaction. The most boring reaction possible. You're a hopeless *median*! And I really thought that you could have been the Seeing-Eye screenwriter for this project."

My panic subsided. I suddenly felt like I was missing out on something vitally important.

"I don't see any problem with me being the screenwriter..."

He broke me off abruptly:

"You are *not* the Seeing-Eye. In this respect you do not suit us at all, unfortunately. But this can still be a fruitful collaboration, just in a different form and on different terms. We'll discuss this, but, please, stop wriggling about in your chair, you're disturbing the people behind you."

Carefully, so that I wouldn't disturb anyone and, most importantly, so that I wouldn't feel my own disgusting jellyishness, I turned my neck and looked behind me. There was another row of red chairs there. And in the chairs there were people.

The woman right behind me had a wet mouth, gaping open, with some horrible white stuff in the corners, and dark, beady eyes. With these beads she was looking dead ahead, right through me it seemed, and swaying slightly from side to side. On her left there was a spotty teenager in glasses, sitting completely still; behind the thick frames, his eyes seemed huge and slightly surprised, but above all vacant. He didn't blink. On the right of the woman was a pale individual with a pasty face, wheezing rhythmically; there were some tubes hanging from his nose... Next to him was a girl. Matted yellow hair, the roots clearly showing. I didn't manage to get a look at the girl's face or the faces of all the other people in the back row because the lights suddenly went out.

The creative director flopped down on the chair next to me and started poking away at the screen of his tablet.

"I would like to offer you the chance to become a member of our fantastic focus group," he whispered confidentially in my ear; his breath smelled of an old chemist's, or maybe seaweed. "I'm sure you'll like it. Great team. Creative work. Important mission. Three meals a day..."

Using his index finger he scrawled some complicated doodle on the screen in Zen Brush mode.

"...But next time you'll have to take a seat in the second row with everyone else. The front row is for the VIP places..."

For a couple of minutes we sat in practically total darkness. All I could see was that silvery rectangle and his index finger tracing the thin black character. Like the signature of a god. Like the footsteps of a pond-skater on the surface of a mercury lake...

And before – yes, before the giant screen in front of us lit up and the creative director put the picture from his tablet up on it, and before he announced the subject of the screening – even before that, I understood the meaning of that great symbol. I suddenly understood it all: that symbol, and the others, and the pain caused by their shape and the fate of those arcing lines, and the essence of their Project.

I applauded, I laughed and I cried, along with the others in the focus group. I was so happy. I whispered in the producer's ear:

"I understand."

"I heard you," the producer said in reply and got up from the chair.

He was leaving – he wanted to leave, but I grabbed him by the shirt and shouted "I understand! I understand!" – until the other guys from the focus group pulled me off.

I am in the focus group. My place is in the second row, third from the right. We get fed three times a day. They bring the food in on these special trolleys, like on an aeroplane. And the plastic containers – they're also the same as on an aeroplane. When I'm eating, I pretend that I'm flying to the moon. My moon is like a round ice floe swimming across the black sky.

Normally they give us spoiled meat, prawns, insects and their grubs. For pudding we get given the infusion.

We sleep wherever. Personally, I sleep right here, in the viewing room. The walkers have their own rooms, they go there at nights.

When night comes, a special signal sounds. Otherwise there would be no way for us to know that the day was over, because the shutters are always down.

Every day we are shown some shots or even whole scenes and we react. The reaction of the focus group is extremely important for the producer and for the director.

I am in the focus group. But I'm capable of more, I'm sure of it. I understand everything. Every day I tell the producer that I understand everything. That I could be the Seeing-Eye. But he doesn't believe me. He doesn't trust me. He says that my place is in the second row, third from the right.

But I'm different. I'm an outlier, I'm not like the others in the focus group. They are all modals. Modals and medians, whatever they might think of themselves. They're blind. They look at the screen and they don't see. I see.

I could be the Seeing-Eye.

I know what is born inside, in the darkness.

## THE PARASITE

We are driving to the main church, past the crowd. Until now we've been living in the TSRC in Kolomna, but Father decided to hold the presentation here. There's still a day to go until the presentation but a queue has already formed – we've been driving through Moscow for two or three hours and the queue is still stretching on behind the metal barriers.

We're in an old minibus with black curtains on the windows and the word 'Ritual' on the side. At first I was surprised. I thought that we'd be led in in triumph, but then I figured out that this was a clever bit of trickery: so that the people in the crowd wouldn't realise who we were and who was with us and so they wouldn't throw themselves under the wheels of the bus.

We're driving at night, but it's still slow because of the traffic jams, so I get to take a good look at that queue. I can see that they're terribly squashed in there, there's not even space to turn around; some of them are standing there limply, their heads hanging down, like horses in a stable, some are pushing and shoving, and others are falling and being trampled and some people are holding out their arms, either to hit them or to pick them up and hug them. I also saw some girl with a big belly trying to get out, to climb over the barrier, but a policeman hit her with a truncheon, right on the belly, when there was probably a little baby in there.

There are lots of policemen on the streets, one standing every ten metres or so. And there are police vans and ambulances along the roads.

When you put it all together it all looks so bad, as if people aren't coming to witness a miracle, but rather that they have something sinister in mind. It's almost like they're not people at all, but a snake with lots of heads that's been caught in a trap to stop it eating the whole city. Someone once told me a story about a snake with lots of heads who attacked a city, but I can't remember it, so I want to think up my own for Pavlusha, while we're driving along, but then Father puts me off by shouting:

"You idiot, shut that curtain!"

No need to shout. They all think that because I can't talk it means I can't hear either, and that I'm an idiot. But I can hear everything, it's just my tongue doesn't do what it's told, that's how the Lord made me – the one they all believe in, or at least pretend to. Myself, I'm not sure if there is a God or not, I've never seen him, and if I ever asked him for something in my prayers he didn't respond and didn't grant my wishes. Maybe I wasn't praying right and he didn't hear me, but Pavlusha always understands me when I'm talking to myself, so I reckon either God doesn't exist or he really doesn't like me and doesn't want me to talk to him. But Pavlusha likes me, he'll only drink water when I give it to him, and he listens to my thoughts and my stories. I tell them in my head and I know that he understands everything.

A few times, when me and Pavlusha were left on our own, he allowed my tongue to move, and I actually said some words – like, "cold" or "hurts" – as if he was talking through me. But that was only after sanitary procedures or when they tried to give him nutrient injections – he won't eat anything we give him – and I stayed back with him to tidy everything up. Pavlusha reacted badly to the jabs – whatever they injected him with, even if it was just glucose, he would screw up his face as if he had a sore tummy and vomit silvery slime. They would leave and I would wipe it up and say to him, in my head: Pavlusha, what's the matter little fellow? it's only glucose, the doctor told us that it's just the same as sugar, it's good for you, you have to eat something, you know... No one else wanted to clean up after him, to touch the thick, shiny puddles – but if you ask me, ordinary vomit or, I don't know, mouse droppings are no better, or worse even, because they stink but this slime of his was like mercury from a broken thermometer and it smelled all eggy and it was quick and easy to wipe up. I would tidy up and he would be cold and or hurting, and he would look at me with his unblinking eyes and he would sing – a humming noise you could only just hear, with his mouth closed, like he was groaning, but very beautiful and melodic. Pavlusha's song was like honey, it flowed into me and filled me with thick, bittersweet amber bliss, and I got a taste in my mouth like when you chew on honeycomb. Then my tongue started to tingle, as if it was being stung, ever so gently, by bees, and I realised that it was Pavlusha, bringing my dead tongue to life with his singing so that I could say a word or even a few words for him.

"...Shut it, do you hear me!" Father roars even louder.

Actually he's not my father at all, my father died of alcoholism a long time ago; he's just a priest in a cassock. But everyone still calls him Father – he insists that they do – and even though I can't say it out loud, I call him that in my head too. In some ways he is like my father – just as loud and mean.

"You cretin, can't you see it's afraid to look outside!?" Father shakes me by the shoulder, then reaches out and is about to shut the black curtain himself when we lurch round a corner. Pavlusha is sent flying forward and Father yanks back his meaty paw, scared that he might accidently brush up against Pavlusha's skin. But what's there to be scared of? I don't understand. His skin is dry and smooth, with a steely shimmer, like a beetle's back. Me, I love beetles. They don't bite.

"He doesn't understand you, Father," the Doctor pipes up from the back seat. "He's deaf and dumb. And *it* gets scared when you shout."

Pavlusha really is stressed out, his eyes have got a violet shine to them. But I think he does want to look out the window, so I don't shut the black curtain. And because I'm upset that they called me "deaf and dumb" and Pavlusha – "it". For some reason they don't use his name. But I think that if that was the boy's name then that name doesn't go anywhere, even if something has happened to the boy... But the Doctor, he really doesn't have a name, the doctors change all the time on our project and I can't learn all of their names. The only one I learned was Vasilevsky, the very first one. He was the one who came up with the project, he was a famous scientist. True, when he was around the project wasn't called "Divine Metamorphosis", just "Metamorphosis". Father joined us later, at the pupa stage. He said that projects like ours could only be run under the aegis of the church, otherwise it would be blasphemy. But Vasilevsky told him that God has nothing to do with it, it's just a scientific experiment, and, he said, you shouldn't go sprinkling my patient with that water of yours, the splashing is bad for the cocoon. I heard this argument with my own ears: I happened to be removing the dead flakes from the cocoon, and they didn't mind me being there, they thought that because I'm dumb that means I'm deaf too, and basically an idiot. But I'm not an idiot. I understood everything. After that Father kicked Vasilevsky off the project, and he kicked off the whole research group as if they'd never existed. He would have kicked me off too – but no one wanted to sleep in the same room as the cocoon anymore and collect the flakes, and I didn't mind. What's more Father thinks that because I'm dumb, it means I won't say anything bad on TV. Not that they would even ask me to be on TV.

Our SRC was renamed a TSRC – that is, a Theological Science Research Centre – whereas before it was just scientific, and not theological. And they put Vasilevsky in prison or something, only no one knows what for, or maybe they do and they won't say. Now we're banned from talking about Vasilevsky; only I can talk about him, in my head, because no one apart from Pavlusha can hear me.

But Vasilevsky, I reckon, he really did want to cure Pavlusha. I remember when they brought Pavlusha in. He was ever so skinny, like he was weightless, and his skin was transparent, with all his veins shining through. Huge blue eyes and golden curls on his head and he smiled so nicely at everyone, like an angel. Pavlusha had some incurable illness, nothing was helping and he was getting worse and worse, so they took him out of the orphanage and brought him to Vasilevsky to be a volunteer, to take part in our experiment and, God willing, get better. I say "our project": actually, at first I had nothing to do with the project. Back then I worked in the Kolomna SRC as a junior lab assistant, looking after all the little test animals – the frogs and the mice and we had some little flies here then too… It was my job to feed the little animals and the insects, to tidy up after them, to clean their cages, and to take away the little dead bodies. Disposal. That's what it was called. I liked my job, except for disposal. The little animals were nice and kind, I would talk to them in my head, give them names, and some of the mice would eat from my hands.

That's how I met Pavlusha: he came to see me to have a look at the little mice. They'd given him the medication already, but the effect wasn't yet visible. He came in every day, he talked to all the rats and the mice, and he talked to me, and he didn't once think that since we – dumb animals – can't reply then that means we can't hear him. There was one mouse that Pavlusha was especially fond of. She said to him "squee-squee-squee", and he said back: "Poor little mousey, don't be afraid, everything's going to be OK, Stepan will look after you." And then he said: "You won't let anyone upset this little mousey, will you, Stepan?" But what could I say in reply, I just moaned, I couldn't even nod, because that would've been as good as lying, because I knew that, if not today, then the next day, they'd take the mouse away from me and then I'd have to dispose of her. So what could I do but not dispose of her, but bury her in the ground – there was nothing else I could do for her. And so I stood in front of him, moaning, and he looked me in the eye and said quietly: "Everything's going to be OK, don't be afraid, Stepan." He had nice eyes then, light blue with dark blue flecks, and eyelashes that were long and curved like a girl's. I looked into those eyes and I believed that everything was going to be OK. And the mouse probably believed that too. It's a shame that Pavlusha doesn't have eyelashes now, and there aren't any flecks in his eyes, now his eyes are so dark and bulbous... And so, he would come every day, always at the same time, when he had some break in his treatment. So when once he didn't come I knew straight away that something was up with my friend Pavlusha, and I headed for the fifth floor where his room was.

They didn't let me in to see Pavlusha then, even though I begged them, and used signs to shown them, and even wrote "Let me in!" on a piece of paper. And that very same day they took Pavlusha's favourite mouse away from me, and three others with her, and later I disposed of those three corpses, but Pavlusha's mouse I buried next to the dump and put a stick in to mark the spot.

A week later Vasilevsky came to see me and gestured to say, "Come with me". And he led me into the room where Pavlusha used to be, and in the hospital bed there was something lying underneath the blanket, but the shape wasn't anything like a body, it was more like a giant egg.

When he saw that blanket, Vasilevsky got incredibly angry and ran straight out into the corridor and shouted at someone for ages:

"Who covered him? Why was he covered? How many times do I have to tell you: the subject is not to be covered!"

A voice mumbled in reply – young, frightened:

"I can't look at it... I, I can't look... and I can't listen to it... you can't through the blanket... all the time there's this bubbling and crunching... I can't... I can't..."

While they were arguing, I quietly took off the blanket – and it really was something like a giant egg lying there, except on the outside there wasn't a smooth shell, but something crimson and lumpy, like a scab – like when you scrape your knee.

Then I remember I pressed my cheek against that crust. If I could have shouted, I would have shouted out: "Pavlusha! What have they done to you?" But my tongue doesn't listen to me, it's been that way since I was born. So I just sat there quietly, pressed up against him, and then I felt my cheek and my ear getting warm, and I felt that he was comforting me from the other side, like before, just without any words. Instead of words I heard the sound of the sea – I've never been to the seaside, but once I was given a seashell to listen to – and in there, under Pavlusha's shell, it sounded just like that, like the waves stroking the sand and whispering a quiet lullaby. Like a butterfly rustling its wings.

I must have dozed off to this lullaby, because I didn't even notice when someone came into the room. I was woken by a woman's voice:

"Aren't you scared to sit there with it? Get out of the way!"

It was Lena, the nurse, she was setting up some device with a little screen next to Pavlusha's cot. Pavlusha had told me about her, he'd said that she was very kind and pretty and that it didn't hurt when she gave him injections. Vasilevsky was standing behind Lena and saying something scientific to her, except he wasn't looking at the screen, but at Lena's neck. She had a beautiful neck, long and slender, like a deer. But then I've never seen a deer, and maybe a deer's neck is completely different, but I've heard that that's what you say about beautiful women. A neck like a deer and eyes like a deer, all frightened. I wanted to say back: why should I be scared, is a seashell scary, or a chicken egg? But as usual I couldn't say anything, so I just moved out of the way like she asked, and moaned and shook my head.

"Is he slow or something?" Lena asked Vasilevsky, and her eyes went mean. I don't know if deer's eyes go like this, but I don't think they do. But I have definitely seen eyes like that before, they belonged to dog with ringworm that used to live in the dump by our SRC. Sometimes I'd throw her some bones, but I never touched her – and rightly so. Later she got rabies and the night watchman killed her and told me to dispose of the body.

"He's dumb," Vasilevsky said. "Maybe I could take him on to look after the pupa… Start the UV scan."

I understood him: the "pupa" is what Pavlusha is now, and I nodded. It was a strange word, gentle somehow, I liked it. I knew what UV was too. They'd done one on me once. It doesn't hurt.

Lena squeezed some see-through syrup out of a tube and started using this smooth thing attached to a sensor to smear it over the surface. The screen was flickering – as if little flies were swarming in there. Lena's face looked like she was going to be sick.

"What's going on in there today?" Vasilevsky asked, and as he did so he covered Lena's hand with his own as she moved the sensor around.

"The same thing," Lena said irritably. "It's the same soup in there."

"Wrong." Vasilevsky took his hand away. "There's more activity today. There's something forming in there…"

"Activity in the soup," Lena said, screwing up her face. "I can't bear touching *it*."

I didn't understand what soup they were talking about and why they thought they could see it. How could they know what was going on in there when it was all closed up? I wanted to tell them that there was something good in there, that there was quiet music playing, the sand and the waves of the sea and the butterflies, that life was being born in there – but I'm dumb, and they were deaf, they couldn't hear the music. I was worried that they'd destroy Pavlusha's "pupa" because they didn't like it, and I moaned in frustration. Vasilevsky shuddered and turned to face me – he'd obviously forgotten that I was in the room too.

"If you want to be with him," Vasilevsky nodded at the pupa, "then stay. Someone has to remove the flakes, keep moisture levels up, measure the surface temperature. And basically make sure that everything's OK."

I nodded.

"The others don't want to go near him, they're afraid. Pavlusha told me that you can hear everything and that you understand, that you only seem like an idiot. So now I'm going to explain to you, as a new participant in the Metamorphosis project, what we're doing here, so that you won't be afraid. Are you going to understand?"

I nodded again, as energetically as possible, so they would have no reason to doubt me. Lena started giggling – at me, obviously. Vasilevsky smiled too for some reason. I don't see what I did that was so funny.

"Many insects produce a special hormone called ecdysone which is responsible for metamorphosis, i.e. for changing them from, say, a caterpillar into a butterfly."

"Or from a maggot into a fly," Lena butted in. Vasilevsky nodded, bent double, like a clown, and continued:

"When the ecdysone starts to be released in place of the previous hormone, the juvenile one, then that launches the transformation mechanism."

I realised that didn't understand what he was talking about any more – not because I'm an idiot, just because I don't know some of words – but I nodded again so they wouldn't work that out. I wanted them to let me be on the project, with Pavlusha.

"...But there are parasites that, once they're inside an insect, 'switch off' the production of ecsydone. So now the opposite happens – the parasite makes the caterpillar produce more and more juvenile hormone, and it grows and grows, increasing in size – but it never forms a cocoon and doesn't turn into a butterfly."

That I understood. I had seen an enormous caterpillar once – that's what had probably happened to it. I groaned so they'd know that I'd heard everything – sometimes people think that I'm deaf too – and the nurse burst out laughing again, and then thrust her hand in the see-through glove between Vasilevsky's legs.

"Say that bit again about it growing and increasing in size," she said, laughing.

"He understood. He's smart," Vasilevsky replied, and I decided that Vasilevsky was a good person and Lena was a bad person. Pavlusha was wrong about her.

"...So, now we're getting to the most important bit. Humans have a gene which is very similar to the gene responsible for the development of ecdysone and metamorphosis in insects – except it's switched off from birth. In crude terms, some parasite has blocked this gene in mankind on a genetic level... The right hormone isn't produced any more and people just keep growing, increasing in size..."

"Increasing in size..." Lena said, stroking his trousers. I was so annoyed – why is this stupid woman getting in the doctor's way when he's talking about science, but Vasilevsky, kind heart, wasn't annoyed at her, but kissed her on the neck and carried on calmly:

"...instead of going through a transformation at puberty. So what we've done is given Pavlusha hormone replacement therapy. He was seriously, terminally ill, anyway. But after the transformation the illness will subside. Right now he is in the cocoon stage."

I got so anxious again because of the words I didn't understand that I started sweating. But I reckoned that I'd still got the main point. I took a notepad and pen out of my pocket – I always carry them with me in case I need to say something important – and wrote: "Will he have wings like an angel?"

Vasilevsky read my question and was delighted at how exactly I'd grasped the essence of his scientific explanation.

"Look at that, eh!" He shook the piece of paper in Lena's face animatedly. "Just look *how much* he understands! How he phrased the question! I mean, see how a person with his intellect is capable of continuing the logical progression: larval – cocoon – winged being...

I was flattered.

"But 'an angel'!" he continued, jumping up and starting to pace around the room. "That's popular consciousness for you, eh! Or rather the subconscious in its purest form. The subcortex! Why are we surprised that people are expecting an angel from us? That all these freaks and holy men are dragging themselves over to see us? It's not just religious fanatics. It's the general populace." Vasilevsky poked me with his finger and I got positively hot with pride. "For the man on the street, person plus wings equals angel."

I shot a look at Lena – I wanted to see the amazement in her eyes, or if not amazement, then at least shame, because now it's clear that I'm not slow, I understand it all just as well or even better than everyone else. But all I could see in Lena's eyes was boredom. It was as if she hadn't even heard what Vasilevsky was saying. She wiped the gel off the cocoon with a whole wedge of paper towels and tried not to touch the surface even with her glove. I motioned to her that I was willing to wipe down the cocoon myself. She looked at me like I was crazy, gave me the paper towels and left.

"We need a mass scientific PR campaign," Vasilevsky continued, either not noticing that Lena had left, or talking to me. "Detailed, objective information about the project in the media and on social networks – none of this medieval hysteria that's everywhere now! All these angels and demons." He raised his voice. "All that nonsense! All that bullshit!" He was already shouting.

I was surprised that Vasilevsky had said a bad word. He's a scientist, an educated man. I didn't understand either why he'd got so angry all of a sudden: he'd only just been praising me. Maybe because I'm wiping down the cocoon without asking him for permission?

I moaned pathetically – yes, I have a specially developed whiney moan to encourage people to pity me – for those times when there's some danger, like someone's going to hit me or take my bag.

Vasilevsky softened instantly and even patted me on the shoulder. He said in a friendly way: "We don't know exactly how the patient is going to look after metamorphosis. But you're right: scientists really do suggest that there will be wings. Except our experiment has nothing to do with angels, or Satan either; it's very important that you understand that."

As I saw it, Vasilevsky was a troubled man, but a good one, I liked him. Because he was kind to me and because he was trying to cure Pavlusha. It's a shame that Father kicked him off the project. It's even more of a shame that they put him in prison. The new doctors never discuss scientific matters with me. They think I'm an idiot. Father didn't sack Lena. People say she wrote a letter against Vasilevsky and also gave Father some Dictaphone recordings on which Vasilevsky badmouths the church. And now she is travelling with us. All fancy, in a dress made of golden scales.

They'd have been better off putting Lena in prison. She doesn't like Pavlusha. She says that Pavlusha's gone and that what he's become isn't Pavlusha anymore, but a monster. She makes his injections painful on purpose, and they don't heal for ages. Pavlusha, when he sees her, is always sad: he remembers that she used to be kind to him. He won't drink water when she offers it to him and he doesn't sing to her.

She's stupid. She doesn't realise what she's missing. No one understands, no one knows. The way he sings! When he sings I'm not just happy. I feel like up to then, before the song, I was dead, and the song has resurrected me, and that while the song is going on, I am alive.

---

The first time I heard Pavlusha's song, he wasn't singing to me. It was three days since he'd come out of the cocoon and they let him outside to have a walk and get some air, under my supervision – because he didn't want to go with anyone apart from me, he started thrashing about and Father was worried that he'd tear his wings – they are very thin, translucent, like on a dragonfly or a fly only bigger. We were both tracked by cameras. And they put a special collar on Pavlusha's neck – if Pavlusha suddenly decides to run off or fly away (although he didn't fly), that collar will give Pavlusha a very painful shock inside, they explained to me, and he won't be able to move for a while.

And so he walked in a circle, slowly, around the main building of the TSRC, and then we stopped by the dump, near where I'd buried the mouse – I'd put a stick in the ground then and it was still jutting out – he stood there and stood there then started singing, not opening his mouth. That's when I heard his sweet howling song for the first time – and felt like I was floating along a river of honey and swallowing the honey and breathing it and the honey was flowing in my veins. But my eyes stayed open, and through the radiant amber haze I saw the stick which I'd put in the ground tremble and fall and then I saw white mouse come out of a heap of rubbish, like its house was in there. I don't know where this mouse came from – maybe it had run away from the lab and started living in the rubbish dump, that happens sometimes – but it was a lot like the mouse that I had buried there once. Her white fur shone. Still singing, Pavlusha picked her up – I could see her whiskers twitching – and then unfurled his translucent wings for the first time. A ray of sunlight reflected in their damp greeny-gold surface, like a fairy-tale lake in a woodland glade, blinding me for a second. I screwed up my eyes, and when I opened them again, Pavlusha was lying unmoving, face down in the rubbish. The collar had kicked in: so he wouldn't fly away.

I picked him up – after the transformation Pavlusha became very light – and carried him into the building. The dead mouse was left sprawling on the rubbish dump. Its rotting brown body teemed with worms and flies. How I could have thought it was alive I don't know.

Since then Pavlusha has never unfurled his wings fully – so he just opens them a bit and flaps them. They've gone dark and are covered in this sort of dust. As he walks along, this dust comes off his wings, like ash from a butterfly singed in a flame.

Now the whole back seat is covered in this dirty-grey dust – I notice it when we finally pull up to the main church and I help Pavlusha get up. On the armrest I find a whole chunk of wing – a soft scrap of Pavlusha's flesh. It's small, about the size of a human fingernail, but it's still a bad sign. He's very weak, he's fading away every day, he's crumbling into dust – and I don't know how to help him.

"Why don't you eat, eh?" I say to him in my head. "Pavlusha, everyone's got to eat." He looks ahead silently with his unblinking eyes covered in a purple film. His eyes are big and bulbous and take up half his face, he doesn't need to turn his head to see me. Why isn't he eating? We've offered him everything we could think of, from pollen to raw beef. He didn't even try them. Maybe the illness that had been killing him before the transformation has come back? Recently I wrote this question on a piece of paper and showed it to the Doctor, but he said no. He said that it couldn't suffer from the illness that that boy had suffered from. The boy had had a blood disease, and it has no blood. As if Pavlusha were someone else.

And now he's fading away, because he doesn't eat.

---

The main church is snow-white, illuminated by spotlights. Around it, as far as the eye can see, there are crowds of people – dark, restless figures swarming all over the square in front of the church and the stairs leading to the entrance, and the bridge, and the river embankment, and the road, and all the surrounding streets. It's as if the church is a cream puff that's been thrown into an anthill. Our ant-trail – from the bus to the doors of the church – is fenced off with metal railings. Inside and outside the barriers, the police form a human chain. They're standing two deep, arms linked, so that we can pass through the crowd untouched.

We walk with Pavlusha in the middle, Father on his right hand, me on the left, and the Doctor, Lena and the rest of the team behind. Pavlusha is covered with a thick blanket to stop anyone seeing him. There are slits cut out of the blanket for his eyes so that he can see where he's going, he mustn't trip up and look ridiculous. Father and I pretend that we're holding him gently by the arm, but in actual fact we're practically dragging him, you can't see from the outside, because no one knows how amazingly light he is. Like a moth.

I'm sure that Pavlusha doesn't like it under the blanket. It's too rough and heavy for his fragile naked body. The crowd is shouting:

"The angel! The angel of the Lord!" They point at Pavlusha. They have icons and pictures of angels. Cherubim, seraphim, archangels. They're yelling and drooling, two women are swaying and shaking their heads in religious ecstasy, someone is choking someone else, a teenage girl's eyes have rolled into her head, foam is coming out of her mouth. They have crucifixes, banners, balloons and Russian flags.

"Praise the Lord! The enemy of the human race, the parasite, has been brought low!"

"And now there is an angel!"

"An angel!"

"My fellow Slavs, fellow Orthodox – rejoice! Orthodox!"

"Long live Russia!"

With each shout Pavlusha shudders and shrinks to one side, but we hold him tight. So tight that I'm afraid we might break something. His limbs are fragile, like plant stems, there are no bones in them, just something like cartilage.

Some woman is holding a picture of a beast with many legs and fangs above her head and screeching hysterically:

"Parasites! We have parasites inside us! From dogs, from cats, from mice, from rats, from pigs, from flies – parasites! And parasites come from the devil!"

Seven women in black headscarves try to break through the chain. They climb over the policemen, screeching and screwing up their faces, as if it were barbed wire; they try to scratch open the policemen's transparent helmets because they can't get to their eyes.

"Let us get to the angel, you beasts, you monsters, you animals! The angel belongs to everyone! It is our right! The angel is for everyone!"

The policemen shove the women to the tarmac, not unlinking their arms, they kick them where they lie. A squat man roars and charges at the policemen, there's something black glistening in his hand, shots are heard, splashes of blood fly toward us, on to Pavlusha's dark blanket. There is a howling in the crowd and, alongside us, the wheezing of the dying. Someone grabs us from behind with strong, rough gloved hands and drags us, not just Pavlusha now, but all of us, including Father, into the church, pushing back the luxurious gilt doors and shutting them behind us.

I pull the blanket off Pavlusha – a cloud of grey dust from his wings rises above us. It looks like nothing's broken. He slowly bends his four legs at the joints and sits on all fours, his hands covering his face. He looks like a crying child right now. But he can't cry, he doesn't have tear ducts.

We hear shouts from outside the door, hissing and shouting. I imagine that it's the many-headed snake hissing and breaking free.

"Tear gas," the Doctor says. He's very pale.

Father, in contrast, is all red. He pants hoarsely.

"Fucking hell. Fanatics."

I'm actually quite pleased at the dirty word. Here, inside the church, it's so unbearably bright and clean, it's so shiny in here, so much gold and electricity, so many candles and icons, that a bit of dirt wouldn't hurt.

"It's too bright in here," the Doctor says, like he's reading my mind. "He'll be very visible. We'll have to turn the lights off during the presentation and just have candles."

"They'll still see him," Father replies. "What a freak, God have mercy on us."

"That's why we're going to put makeup on him," Lena joins in. "We're going to make everything look as good as possible."

This is the first I've heard about makeup, they haven't discussed it in front of me before. I pull the notebook out of my pocket so I can write "No makeup" but I've dropped my pen out there, in the crowd. You mustn't put makeup on him. There's all those chemicals in it, and he has such thin skin, you mustn't.

"What are you moaning about?" Father wrinkles his red face. "Shut up, idiot."

He takes a long and unpleasant look at Pavlusha – as if he were a beetle that he's caught and he can't decide what to do with him: tear off his legs, chop him in two, or just squash him, so he doesn't suffer, that would be kinder. He clearly has no intention of letting the beetle go.

When we were leaving the TSRC I had let all the little animals go. The frogs, mice, rats and flies. And I didn't get in any trouble because I'm a member of the project. And I would have let Pavlusha go too, and I would have gone with him – he wouldn't manage without me, he needs to be looked after – but they never take that terrible collar off. And Father keeps the remote control on him. They say that it's built into his cross.

"We've got about a day before he's done for," Father pronounces finally. "We have to present him to the public tomorrow morning."

"But it's all been arranged..." the Doctor objects uncertainly. "Both the VIPs and..."— he points upwards, at the dome of the church — "and the leadership have been invited for the day after tomorrow."

"And what are we going show them the day after tomorrow – a corpse?"

Father screeches. "Or, perhaps, we should show them our fucking dicks?"

More words spat out like dirty spittle on a candle. I wouldn't use dirty words if I could talk...

"He's not going to last until the day after tomorrow, just look at him," Father continued, more calmly.

You're lying, you're lying, I say in my head. Pavlusha isn't dying. Pavlusha, don't die, don't listen to him...

"We'll warn the VIPs that the presentation is going to be earlier. Due to popular demand. We'll say the people can't wait any longer, there's already been a homicide by the church. Or something along those lines."

"OK," says the Doctor.

Father scowls: he doesn't like the word "OK"; for him it's dirtier than "dick".

"So be it," the Doctor corrects himself. "We also still need to decide how the people are going kiss him during the veneration. On the foot? Or the wing? Or the hand?"

"Not the wing, their lips will get covered in that crap. And the hand doesn't work either – too close to the face, they'll see him. The feet would be better. The hind legs. We'll let them in in two lines, they can kiss the left and the right. And the middle one we'll have to tie up and hide under the costume. Because angels don't have six limbs. Six wings ma-a-a-ybe..." Father twisted his mouth in a broad yawn and crossed it with his hand. "Go on then, Lena, get the makeup girl and start right away."

You can't start right away! I shout in my head, but no one apart from Pavlusha can hear me, all they hear is hear moaning. "You mustn't. Pavlusha needs sleep, he's tired."

"Shut up," Father says, not even looking in my direction. "I'm going to have a little rest."

He crosses the church and disappears behind the altar. The makeup artist comes – it's the girl who was in the bus with us: I was surprised that I hadn't seen her on the project before.

⁂

They do Pavlusha's make up in a special room. There are no icons in here, although there is a mirror covering one wall, and a big TV on the other one. And a black leather sofa, which they told me to sit on. At first they didn't even want to let me in, but Pavlusha started fighting, thrashing about and shaking his wings to make them let me stay with him – they were afraid that if they didn't he'd die right there and then.

The make-up room smells of the cold skin of dead animals and Pavlusha's warm, stuffy fear. The floral fragrances of the make-up can't drown it out. Pavlusha's fear smells of wormwood and putrid bogs, of autumn mushrooms and rotten leaves and birds' eggs that have been out in the sun too long, and, for some reason, of blood. But the Doctor said he doesn't have any blood.

But on the outside Pavlusha is calm – the nurse injected him with a sedative to stop him squirming. The girl that was supposed to do Pavlusha's make-up was taken away: she felt sick when she touched Pavlusha's skin. I don't know what makes them so squeamish. Their own skin is much more disgusting. They have spots and wrinkles and blackheads and grease. But Pavlusha's skin is all clean and smooth and neat...

There's another man instead of the girl. He was brought in especially in a car with a siren. Normally he does the makeup for corpses in the morgue – the ones that have been in car accidents and so on and their faces are all messed up. They got him to come because he wouldn't be scared of Pavlusha. For him Pavlusha's the same as a corpse.

But Pavlusha is alive; I can see how much it hurts when the cosmetologist puts white paint on his transparent wings.

Daybreak. Lena clicks the remote control, the TV comes on. On the morning news they're saying that the presentation of the Divine Metamorphosis project will take place at midday today. They show the happy faces of the people crowding outside our church. They don't mention the casualties on this channel, but Lena turns on another one, a foreign one. I don't understand what they're saying, but on the screen there are bloodied bodies on stretchers and on the pavement, and our church in the background.

They want to stick white feathers on top of the paint on Pavlusha's wings. But you mustn't! I shout in my head. A layer of paint and feathers is too heavy for such thin wings, they won't take the weight. Pavlusha shrinks into himself, folding his wings shut like an accordion, but they force them open. Lena holds the wing and the cosmetologist glues the feathers on. Pavlusha bends double and vomits silvery slime, some drops fall on the scales of her dress. Lena screams and hits Pavlusha in the face. He covers his face with his hands, but I manage to see that the thin, shiny skin on his cheek is torn and transparent droplets, like tears, are coming out of the wound.

I clean up after him, mop the silvery slime from the floor and wipe the eggy-smelling drops from the scaly fish dress, and all this time these drops are dripping from his cut onto the floor. And I realise that he doesn't have tears in his eyes because they fill his whole body – they're what he has instead of blood.

The cosmetologist paints Pavlusha's huge eyes blue, and Lena flicks the remote control again, changing the channels. Pavlusha looks into the mirror with his new blind blue eyes, and the mirror reflects the TV on which Father is looking down at him.

It's a repeat of one of the talk-shows that Father's been on, they've been showing a lot of them recently. Father is sitting in an armchair in a circle of white light, content and glossy, with his big cross on his stomach. In another armchair – around which there is another circle of light, but much fainter – is the Doctor, not the one that's on the project now, but the one before him. And in the third chair, plunged into darkness, is the presenter. You can barely see his face and his voice sounds goatish.

"It's your assertion that some parasite has, on a genetic level, for many millennia, been preventing mankind from developing according to our true nature?"

"Our true divine nature," Father corrects him grandly.

"We definitely want to hear your thoughts on that, Father, but this question is to the man of science."

"Yes, that is our assertion," the Doctor says indecisively.

"So the parasite is a sort of check, a safeguard?"

"You could say that."

"So, we could well suggest that this 'safeguard' preventing transformation was not sent by Satan, but by God, to stop people from becoming animals? What is your basis for asserting that your creation, post-metamorphosis, is divine and not satanic?"

...The cosmetologist smears foundation all over Pavlusha's face and body – he's trying to give his skin a boyish pinkness. Pavlusha trembles. His skin turns the fake pink colour of a Chinese plastic doll.

On the TV, the terrified Doctor says nothing, looking down from the screen at us in fear, at Pavlusha – as if he were waiting for him to give a hint. They show the Doctor's face in close up; dark drops of sweat are forming on his forehead like acne.

"If I may, I'll come to my colleague's assistance." On the screen Father smiles, but I know that smile, he's absolutely furious. "A 'parasite sent by God' is simply impossible, it's heresy. The parasite is the enemy of mankind, and now we've found a way of fighting it!" The audience bursts into applause. Father holds the pause patiently. "Our creation, as you chose to call him, is a creature pure, meek and free from sin."

"What about how he looks?" the presenter bleats. "Does he look like an angel?"

"It's not for me to say," Father replies strictly. "But when the metamorphosis was complete and our Pavel appeared, I realised that I had already seen him before, in the paintings of the Italian masters of the Renaissance."

...The cosmetologist glues a wig of golden curls to Pavlusha's smooth head. He and Lena pull his middle legs up against his body and wind twine round them. Pavlusha doesn't resist. They put a shining robe on him. Pavlusha's skin makes him looks like Punch in a puppet show. I can sense how much he is suffering under the layers of paint, synthetic material, glue and feathers.

I go over to the window so that, at least for a minute, I don't have to see what they have done to him.

"And what does he eat?" I hear the presenter's voice.

I look down, into the crowd. They're fighting, tearing and biting at each other – like dogs scrapping over a bone thrown by their master. They're getting mauled and trampled. The VIP corteges drive straight through the crowd, crushing anyone who does not or cannot get out of the way.

"It would not be an exaggeration to say that he is nourished by the Holy Spirit," Father says on the TV. "He drinks water, and that's it."

Just sing, Pavlusha, I say to him in my head. Sing, that's the most important thing. I don't know what else can help you.

When the doors to the church are opened at midday and the many-headed snake bursts in, I realise that they won't accept him. He doesn't look like the pictures of angels they have with them. Under a layer of paint and foundation – an interloper, an alien; under the feathers – ash. And the badly stuck on white feathers are already crumbling off his wings.

Pavlusha is on a dais, daubed in paint and silent, in the light of the candles. His golden robe hides a pair of extra limbs and the collar on his neck. Now they're coming to kiss his feet – when they get a sight of him, they'll tear him to pieces. At the moment their faces are twisted in love and ecstasy – in a minute they will be grimaces of disgust and hate.

Their mouths are open wide, shouting ecstatically, and this shouting drowns out the welcoming speech which Father had spent so long preparing.

"Brothers and sisters... The hour has come... Let us rejoice... The enemy of mankind... A moment of your time, please...! Our project is unique... We have cast down..." From time to time Father's voice emerges from the roiling foam of their shouting. But they have no intention of listening to Father, they want to hear the angel. Father fiddles irritatedly with his huge cross. In this cross, on the reverse, there are special buttons which control the collar on Pavlusha's neck. In case he suddenly tries to fly away.

But he doesn't. Through blue-painted eyes Pavlusha looks meekly into the crowd. Just sing, I say to him in my head. When you sing, miracles happen. They will forgive you, if only you sing!

He hears me. Not opening his mouth, barely audibly, he takes up his sweet song. It is like the rustling wings of a butterfly, like a gentle sigh.

Sing, sing! When you sing, we, born in sorrow, remember the bliss of our mother's womb. When you sing, honey flows from men's nipples and women collect it in warm honeycombs.

And he sings. His song is like a moan of love and pain.

Don't stop, sing louder, or you'll die! When you sing, the old become young and the dead are filled with life...

Now Pavlusha has opened his mouth and is singing louder and louder. So loudly that his song can be heard in all corners of the church. His breathing is like buzzing, his groaning like the humming of a thousand insects. His song is more beautiful now than ever. I can feel it sting my dead tongue, bringing it to life.

And then, shouting over the crowd, shouting over his song, I say:

"Everyone be silent and listen."

My voice is strong and pure. Everyone falls silent. But Pavlusha sings.

I go over to Pavlusha and tear off his wig and golden robe. I go over to Father and tear off his cross.

"Let him go," I order Father. He presses the button obediently, and the collar falls from Pavlusha's neck. He unhurriedly unfolds his wings, white feathers circling in the air.

His mouth is like a dark trumpet through which he trumpets his song. His mouth is like the proboscis of a giant horse fly. In the depths of the proboscis I can see thin black needles.

Then I say to the crowd:

"On your knees."

They all kneel down, but I stand alongside him.

Let him take their blood and drink his fill, I do not pity them. He has gone hungry for so long.

## THE BORDER

In the end they had ordered standard sleeper tickets. Olga, of course, had wanted first class, but the prices shot up for the school holidays and first class there and back would have used up all of Okhotin's wages for February, and they had to have something to live on when they got back... Properly speaking, on their budget, they should have gone economy, in the open sleeper car. Okhotin had even vaguely suggested something along those lines, but Olga shot him a look as if he'd just told a bad joke or his stomach had rumbled or something and said:

"Economy is for poor people."

She said it quietly, but with a nasty tinny rattle in her voice. Okhotin frowned. In the last few years she had developed this habit of making these announcements all the time, categorical and spiky, like the scratch of a cupronickel fork on a dirty plate.

"Forty-six years old and he doesn't earn enough to get decent tickets," Olga clanked away again. "If first class is too expensive then it's the standard sleeper or not at all."

"OK, OK, we'll get a sleeper cabin, don't worry," Okhotin snapped back wearily. Saying "All right then, we're not going at all" would have meant a repeat of last week's discussion of how and where they'd be going – that is, two women being hysterical. One tantrum had been viscous and poisonous, like mercury, before going into a smouldering phase – Olga's; the other came with floods of tears and snivelling, as well as door-slamming and the inevitable asthma attack at night – Dasha's. But the main reason he agreed was that *he* wanted to go.

He really wanted to go. He missed her.

...The conductors were well trained and welcoming in a forced way, with their starched white shirts and old-fashioned jackets the colour of spoiled cherries.

"Good evening, are you three all travelling together?" said one of the conductors, his face dawning into a cheery smile. There was a little badge on his chest: "Dmitry Shmarov: All-time great conductor."

"Not exactly," Olga replied cheerlessly, holding out three passports and tickets. "My husband is getting off earlier."

"Well how about that!" Shmarov's delight became even more intense. "Any coffees or teas before we set off?"

"Three teas with lemon," Olga said wearily.

"Two teas," Okhotin corrected her. "And a cappuccino for me, please."

Olga glared crossly at her husband, but said nothing. "Do you always have to make such a song and dance about being *different*?" her look said. Okhotin made a face of dumb surprise. As if to say, I'm not making a song and dance. I just like coffee.

"I can bring you three teas and one cappuccino, if you like." The "All-time great conductor" valiantly threw himself on the grenade.

"Yes, thank you," Olga said.

"No, there's no point," Okhotin said and, barely visibly, shrunk his head into his shoulders. "I don't want tea."

All in all it was a decent train, nice and clean, but there was a glittering suspension of dust swirling in the corridors. Dasha sneezed a few times.

"Take a puff!" Olga handed Dasha an inhaler. "You getting wheezy is the last thing we need!"

Dasha gripped the oval mouthpiece in her lips drowsily and took a puff.

A gaggle of three teenage boys in black leather jackets made their way through the carriage, crunching and jangling. An old woman with a clownish mop of raspberry-coloured hair trotted behind them warily; a minute later she came back and spent an age standing in the door checking her ticket, sighing and shuffling about, before finally coming inside.

"I'm in six," she announced sorrowfully. "The top bunk... Oh dear, the top bunk..." She clutched her lower back demonstratively. "Now, perhaps, if the gentleman..."

The old lady fixed her faded mole-like eyes on Okhotin, expectantly.

"Why don't you take my bunk?" Okhotin responded readily; again, Olga shot him a look of contempt. She had made a *special effort* to get the lower bunks. Ungrateful and inconsiderate.

The cappuccino turned out to be extraordinarily disgusting, and Okhotin regretted not agreeing to a tea. Olga put some sugar in her cup and gave it a long and enthusiastic stir. She took a sip – and then started up the same old tune again. That all *normal* people go on holiday as a family, we're the only ones who, for some reason, have to do it differently, who, for some reason, go separately... The old dear with the raspberry hair nodded sympathetically in time with Olga's speech.

"You could join me," Okhotin responded dutifully. "I've got nothing against taking you with me."

"Nothing against it!" Nevertheless Olga snapped back. "He's got nothing against taking us to see *that girl of his*. No, thank you very much. Once was enough for me."

... Six months ago Olga had taken the trip with him. After that she had started referring to "*that girl of yours*". At first Okhotin had been amazed at this and had tried to prove that she was being crazy – how can you get jealous in a situation like this?! Later he was hurt and angry and begged Olga not to call her that – but recently he'd come to terms with it. It's true, they are very different people. This woman here, and that one there. *That* one he loved. *This* one he pitied and tolerated...

"...I don't want to go with Daddy either!" Dasha piped up capriciously. "I want to go really far. Really far, like you said! And in a plane next time. You promised!"

New Rail and the Air Force had divided up the routes strictly: the trains went *back*, slowly, like in the good old days, choo-choo, and the planes went *forward*, on towards the bright future. True, people were even saying that soon you'd be able to travel directly, without any illusions, but Okhotin didn't believe it. Transportation without a means of transport and it's next stop insanity. A psychotherapist friend of Okhotin's was, incidentally, in complete agreement.

...They had indeed been promising Dasha for ages that she could get the plane in the summer. With the rest of her class. She'd thrown a tantrum back then too, she'd wanted to go by plane, but he and Olga had refused categorically. They'd already all taken a flight together twice – the first time a hundred years forward, the next as far as five hundred years forward – and both times Dasha had been utterly thrilled, but they hadn't liked it. It was depressing and creepy and they couldn't get the hang of the language at all... They'd had to buy Dasha off with the promise that on this trip they'd take the train really far back.

"As long as it's something educational." Olga stated her conditions. "Something informative."

While Dasha was looking through the "educational" catalogue, Okhotin plucked up courage and confessed to his wife that, personally, he didn't want to go that far back. And that, in fact, he didn't want to go somewhere new at all.

"You see, I'm too old now for new places really," he said. "I'm like a pensioner, you know… I want to go back to where I've already been… Where I'm guaranteed to enjoy it…"

"Guaranteed," Olga repeated the word with venom and got ready to cry. "So, with *that girl of yours* it's guaranteed…"

…The conductor finally brought in the silvery capsules and bottles of water on a battered square tray. He gave them the standard forms to sign (I, Mikhail Okhotin, passport number etc etc, am aware of the possible complications…); he had a plastic smile which ran the length of his jaw:

"Just a formality."

The loudspeaker came on with a damp grunt, and gave a cheerful update from the ceiling:

"New Rail and Zeitgeist International Ltd would like to welcome you on board the Prince Vladimir. Please remember that before their journey begins, all passengers must swallow their individual capsules with an appropriate quantity of water and adopt a comfortable position. We would like to request that non-ticket-holders please leave the train. Have a safe and pleasant journey!"

…As usual, two minutes or so after the capsule, they set off. The raspberry-haired old lady immediately started rustling through plastic bags and tin foil, laying out some cold chicken on grease-soaked napkins. The smell of garlic-flavoured meat spread through the compartment – but then Okhotin checked himself sharply: there is no smell, damn these bloody reflexes! What are they like these people, he thought irritatedly when the smell had disappeared obediently … they're on this spiritual journey, their minds transported, and all they've got on their mind is a dead chicken…

Olga made up her bed straight away and lay down to sleep facing the wall. Dasha kept digging through her girly soft-pink rucksack (what is it with women and their obsession with bringing as much stuff as possible when in actual fact you don't need *anything at all*?). Finally, from somewhere at the very bottom, she pulled out a guide to the Early Palaeolithic with a beetle-browed Neanderthal on the cover and took it up with her to the top bunk. The thought struck Okhotin that the Neanderthal bore a distinct resemblance to a neighbour of theirs, the idiot Tolyan from the second floor…

"Oh, so you're whatsit, off to see the ancestors, are you?" The raspberry-haired old dear ran her eyes over the guidebook enviously. Rudely, Dasha said nothing back. As ever, Okhotin felt awkward on her behalf.

"My wife and daughter are off to the Paleolithic, yes," Okhotin responded politely. "But I'll be getting off earlier, in '88…"

And then he added, as if apologising:

"I spent my youth there…"

"I'm off in '03, March," the old lady informed him eagerly and gnawed at a chicken bone. She was clearly waiting for Okhotin to ask her a question.

"Why so close?" Okhotin asked with obedient surprise, although he had absolutely no interest in the answer.

"I'm off to whatsit, the wake," the old lady explained cheerfully. "That was the year my husband passed on…"

"So why are you going to the wake?" Now Okhotin was genuinely surprised. "You could go back a bit further and he'd be alive?"

"Hmm, alive…" the old lady hesitated strangely. "Alive they scare me, it's whassisname… But like this, to mark his memory, it's whassisname, it's right and proper, it's the way I like it…"

The raspberry-haired old woman said something else. Okhotin wasn't listening, but he nodded politely, and when he'd had altogether enough, he went out of the compartment and into the corridor, where he pressed his hot face against the glass. For some reason, it suddenly felt uncomfortable, fake or something. Then he figured it out: "The glass should be cold." And the glass went cold.

And so he stood there, looking at images of the late Noughties flashing by outside the window, in the grey drizzle: boring shopping centres, boring traffic jams for mile after mile, boring people… He stood there and thought about Olga. That Olga, the young one, the one he loved, the one from the Eighties… Recently he'd started going to see her a lot in May '88. A good time. A spring of pervading tenderness that smelled of grass, streams and cats. She's nineteen. She still lives with her parents. In her second year at university. In a year's time they'll meet. In three they'll marry. In six, in '94, there'll be the miscarriage — and the dimples will disappear from her cheeks. In ten, in '98, Dasha will arrive — and Olga will start to frown and raise her voice. And she'll stop being his Olga — that Olga — forever. But that's not for a long time yet. She doesn't know that all this is going to happen. She doesn't know why she dreams of a strange man at night. In six months' time, on their first date, she'll tell him, giggling bashfully, that "it's fate". That, before they met, she had seen him in her dreams. But in those dreams he seemed much older... On that first date he won't understand her or believe her (although he'll pretend that he does). He'll understand later, much later, when she puts on weight and becomes this Olga. When Zeitgeist International starts these journeys and when, for the first time, he travels to the spring of '88 and can't resist it and breaks the rules and enters her dreams. And he initiates contact — although contact is banned — and goes too far. He loves her at night but in the day he is *present but unseen*, like you're supposed to be...

"Oh dear Lord!" The raspberry old lady came speeding out of the cabin and stood next to Okhotin. "Just as long as there's no Border today, Lord deliver us!"

"There won't be a Border," Okhotin said with a patronising smile.

"God willing, God willing..."

"There is no Border. Those are just superstitious rumours."

The old dear retreated quietly into the cabin, nodding doubtfully at Okhotin. Okhotin swore in irritation. All these bloody grannies and granddads. Who dreamed up this Border out of boredom and then go and believe in it themselves. Look what they've gone and done with this old-wives tale of theirs! They can't just go about their journey quietly, mentally scoffing their chicken. No — there's this Border. So let's all get scared and have a good old worry about getting thrown off. In an endless field, in the middle of nowhere. With no explanation. And the train keeps going.

The old granny got off in 2003: for some reason Okhotin felt sad when he saw her wandering through the spring mud towards the blue and white high-rises, off to start her mourning.

...*alive they scare me*...

What's there to be scared of? That's happiness – the living!

...As he was pondering this, the concrete barriers of the lawless Nineties stretched on outside the window. And the Nineties themselves — messy and flavoursome, with dirty windows. The smell of sweat and petrol and skin and gunpowder. Kiosks, stalls, bins, building sites, brothels, bars... Darkness fell quickly.

Choking on their snorts of laughter, jangling metallically and munching on crisps, the three teenagers in black jackets moved past Okhotin and unloaded onto the platform at '94. They took a little look around. And then sullied the already dirty tarmac with sticky gobbets of young spit. So: they've pitched up to take a look at the crazy days of the Nineties. To be *present but unseen*...

...On their way into the Eighties something happened. They braked, pulling up with a screech. They were sitting there for ages, half an hour or an hour, in the middle of the dark night. Okhotin was bored. His wife and daughter were asleep, knitting their identical gingerish brows… Then the train seemed to get going again — but sort of slowly, rocking side to side... And then they came to a standstill again. The cabin became stuffy.

Okhotin tried to imagine that the air was fresh, but for some reason it didn't work. He tugged at the window — nailed shut. He wandered over to the conductors to ask what was going on and how long they'd be stopping for — but their compartment was locked and they didn't respond to his knocking. He went back. He pressed his face up against the glass, trying to pick out the landscape outside the window through the greasy smears. Darkness, darkness… Some abandoned station with a single shining streetlight and darkness — flat and boring, all the way to the horizon…

…Suddenly, just behind him, he heard someone's rapid, fetid breathing. He turned around — slowly, like in a dream — and saw a dog. Huge, pointy-eared and black, first it sniffed Olga, who lay there motionless, and then him, Okhotin, his trousers and shoes: its jaws were wet with saliva and the sweet odour of carrion.

Okhotin sat down. He didn't like dogs, he was afraid of them. There was a sickening spasm in his stomach. Lucky I've got my travel nappies on, Okhotin thought.

"Who do you belong to, doggie?" he whispered ingratiatingly and peered over at Olga. She was still sleeping, her breathing quiet and even. Then she suddenly pulled her head up strangely and let out a long scream.

Okhotin screwed up his eyes and tried to get the dog out of the cabin. The way they'd been taught at Zeitgeist's travellers' courses: "I cannot see this object, I do not believe in this object." I do not believe, I do not believe, I do not believe… It seemed to work. The scream broke off with a hoarse honking noise, and the sweet smell disappeared.

Okhotin swallowed quietly and carefully and opened his eyes. A man in fatigues was standing in the door to the compartment.

"Mikhail Okhotin?" the man asked mournfully.

"Yes, that's me…"

"Good evening, border control. Please make your way off the train."

Okhotin felt his travel nappy fill with something warm.

"Good…" he squeezed out. "What… control? On what grounds?"

*I cannot see this object I do not believe in this object I cannot see this object I do not believe in this object…*

"We have the right to remove passengers at the border without explanation."

"But this must be… there's been some kind of… mistake… some misunderstanding." Okhotin looked imploringly into the guard's eyes, which were small and dull, the colour of damp earth.

*something's wrong*

"There's been no mistake," the guard said wearily. "No misunderstanding."

*there's something wrong with his eyes*

"Please make your way out of the compartment. Out of the carriage. Off the train."

*they're not moving. they're like little rubber stickers. they're not blinking at all*

"Olga… Olga!" Okhotin gave out a strangled sob. "Dasha!"

"They can't hear you."

"Why can't they hear me?" Okhotin asked, his lips numb.

"Every passenger is on his own journey."

"I'm not getting off." Okhotin lay down hurriedly and pulled the itchy blanket, encrusted with brown patches, up to his chin.

"So we're going to have to make you." The guard's upper lip quivered and crawled up towards his nose, exposing his long teeth. "Without explanation."

"Dmitry, get in here!" The all-time great conductor bent over the traveller.

The traveller was lying on the floor, his head jammed against a metal table leg. The other three — the woman, the girl and the old lady — were lying on their bunks and breathing well, evenly.

"Has he been like that for long…?" Dmitry asked stupidly.

"How would I know?!" his colleague said angrily.

It was five hours since the Prince Vladimir was shunted down a dead-end siding — and about three hours since the two colleagues moved from beer to vodka.

"Has he got a pulse?" Dmitry squatted down, holding up the tails of his jacket so they wouldn't get stained, and grasped the traveller by the wrist. "Doesn't seem to. Go on, call an ambulance. Looks like the same as last week…"

"These effing blokes with dodgy hearts, why do they come on here when they know full well the pressure it puts on your heart!"

"What's that got to do with it…?" Dmitry said scornfully. "He probably just wasn't let across the Border."

"Not you as well. What bloody border might that be, Dmitry?!"

"The Border exists," Dmitry responded stubbornly. "The chief conductor said so. They take people off without explanation…"

After the train had disappeared from view, Okhotin shifted chillily from one foot to another.

An endless field stretched away in all directions.

## GREEN PASTURES

Everyone thinks that on death row you get fed the whole time. That in here you get given fruit, nuts, caviar, chocolate, sugar-oxygen cocktails… That they're fattening you up for the kill, that's what everyone says. I even used to think that myself once. And I used to think: how can people stuff themselves if they're about to be killed? How do they keep it down? Why do they agree to stuff themselves, to make all this effort for the people that are going to live on after them? Alisa and I even made a pact once: if we ever do get sentenced for some reason… Not, of course, that we were planning on committing a crime – it's just everyone knows that you can be given a max for any old shit, some people even say that the judges have a quota – X number of maxes in a year… But, of course, we didn't really think that that sort of thing could happen to us – we made a pact just in case: we'd refuse any food or water, go on hunger strike and completely starve ourselves so that we'd die before they could get their hands on us, or in the first few days afterwards, which would be even more annoying for them. Or no one would like the look of our sick, haggard bodies. And we thought too that we'd be able pluck up our courage and just kill ourselves – if you want to you can kill your body with a spoon. Or you could easily choke yourself on that chocolate they give you, or on an apple core…

But now it's happened to us for real. And here I am in a cell, and Alisa's here too somewhere, in a cell on another floor or in another prison even, or maybe she's already gone, and all our pacts were just naïve nonsense. We were ignorant, pig ignorant. I wonder, are pigs really ignorant? Where does that expression come from? Maybe because they don't know that they're going to be sent to the abattoir? That from morning to night they're being fattened up to be slaughtered?

In actual fact you don't get fed here at all, at least not in the normal sense of the word. A tube down your throat – force-feeding, overseen by a doctor, twice a day. Vitamins and glucose, sure, but not from fruit and not from chocolate. I get all my nutrients in the form of injections. So there can be no forks, or spoons, or little bones which I could use to do something to myself.

And everything is soft in here, in this death-row cell, soft and springy like a baby's play-pen. The floor is soft, the walls are soft. God forbid I fall and hurt myself. God forbid I start running headfirst into the wall.

They took my clothes and didn't give me any others. Who knows what might happen, I could strangle myself or figure out something else. And they have climate control in here, in this cell – the perfect temperature and humidity. My overseer even said: "Don't worry, you won't catch a cold here." Ever so polite. And I didn't know whether he was making fun of me or not. Maybe he really did think I was worried about catching a cold. They're thick, the overseers. But very healthy. People say that many of them are disconnected to order, "fenced" on the sly, right here in the prison operating theatre, and they haven't got a clue why they get asked in…

It suits everyone better that I'm naked. I can't hide anything from the cameras and the doctors can make an instant evaluation of the condition of my body, of my skin… On the first day I told them that I was embarrassed, I asked them to give me something to cover myself, some pants or at least a loincloth or something. The nurse – she's so fat and ugly, no risk of her ending up in the operating room – just snorted: "It doesn't bother any of us." And she looked at me like I was a corpse in a morgue asking for pants. Because, of course, to her I'm already dead, and corpses don't need to hide their nakedness.

So, when the doctor comes – I'm naked. The cameras watch me – I'm naked. The lawyer says I might have a chance at an acquittal – and I sit there naked and listen. It feels like I'm in a dream, that dream that you've come to work with no trousers on. And everyone's looking at you and you're ashamed and scared… Why, by the way, is having no clothes on so terrifying in dreams?

The only thing I am wearing are these special coverings on my fingers and a mouthguard on my teeth. So I can't scratch or bite myself. So I don't damage myself in any way. There's a nasty taste in my mouth from the mouthguard – but I've pretty much got used to it already. It still makes me lisp a bit – but I've got no one to talk to really, except the lawyer, and he doesn't care whether I can pronounce my esses or not.

My lawyer says that there's a chance I could get a reduced sentence, or even an acquittal. He says that he's sent the case for review and that there'll be a verdict soon. And that there's no reason for me to panic, why am I getting so worked up, we live in a just, transhumanist society, people don't get sentenced to a maximum for just any old thing. And I'm better off just keeping my head down and not giving them any reason to complain, offering up my veins for the injections I need, I mean, really, what's the problem, I'll be healthier myself and then they'll put me in an ordinary cell or even let me go. I just need to forget all these scare stories about judges having quotas. He talks and talks…

He seems like an OK guy, the lawyer. Young, a boy still really, not inhabited by the looks of it. He doesn't look at my nakedness. He's the only one who turns away… He wants to comfort me, I realise, he wants to give me hope. It's not likely he's such an idealist – although, as far as I can tell, this is his first case. Sometimes I so want to believe what he's saying that I almost do believe. But he leaves and the fat nurse comes and force feeds me from a tube, and once again I know that the end has come.

There are too many of them. Too many on the waiting list.

⁂

There are too many of them. Demand is significantly higher than supply. That's what the woman at the local Human Plus office said. A couple of months ago Alisa and I went there to sign up for digitisation. It was Alisa's decision. She said that we were never going to be happier than we were at that moment, so it was a good time to get a CD and we needed to seize the moment.

At first we liked the place – it was clean and natural. A whole meadow full of ears of green, long-haired corn and beyond the meadow a pond and in the pond the reflection of the "millstones" of Human Plus – their building is shaped like a windmill. Alisa and I walked through the meadow, holding hands and imagining that one day, many years later, there would be only one person walking here, but it would still be us. We tried to imagine what it would be – a girl or a boy. And Alisa laughed and said it should be a boy because she'd like to have a proper cock. And I argued with her and said "a girl would be better", but just because, as a joke, I didn't really mind. The important thing is we'd be together. We imagined what our body's hair would be like, its eyes, skin, ears. And then we started to wonder what would happen to the bodies we have now.

"Well, first we're going to live until we're old," Alisa said. "And then when our bodies are completely wrinkly and gross…"

"And when they can no longer fuck each other."

"Yeah, when they can no longer fuck, and when we finish paying off our implantation mortgage at that exact same moment, we'll bring them down here and they'll implant us in some great young guy, and these bodies…" — she looked down at her feet, then nervily looked me up and down, then turned round, as if she was about to give us both away — "they'll burn them, I guess. Or bury them somewhere round here. And we'll… They will fertilise the wheat. Or the, whatever, oats."

Squinting, she looked up at a bird circling unhurriedly above the meadow. Then she said quietly: "He maketh me to lie down in green pastures."

"What are 'pastures'?" I asked. "Who is 'he'? What is that anyway?"

"Don't you like it?" she said, hurt.

"No, I like it, I just don't get what it means."

"I don't get it either. But I don't think you have to. It's a line from some poem, I heard it when I was little. Pastures… I think pastures are something like this meadow. With birds flying overhead."

…But then we started to like the place a lot less. Because we were standing by the entrance for a really, really long time, like beggars, explaining who we were to a rude voice in a loudspeaker that demanded we show some pass or other and that kept saying that Human Plus was closed to visitors that day.

About twenty minutes later, and only after Alisa banged her hand against the bars a couple of times and made a show of blowing on her palm, and after I'd said that if he didn't let us in at once then we'd climb over the fence and if we hurt ourselves he'd be the one responsible for reckless body usage, not us, because, as a public service, Human Plus is obliged to receive people during its opening hours and, as the security guard, he is obliged to let them — that is, us — in, and if then it turns out that he just drove us to despair, then he'd be to blame for the injuries… Basically, only after we'd threatened him a bit did the electric gates open, and then we spent ages wandering round the grounds looking for the right building, and then looking for the right floor, and then the right office… And then this woman with a froglike smile said that she wouldn't register us for Consciousness Digitisation.

"You haven't understood," Alisa said. "We'd like to take out a mortgage on CD and implantation into the same body. With a forty-year fixed term, on the Young Family scheme. We just got married."

She showed her our certificate.

"Congratulations," — the frog's smile got even broader — "but there's nothing I can do to help."

"What do you mean 'nothing'? It said on your site that there's this scheme 'Young Family: Two in One'. It said on there that it's a low-cost option in cases of a body shortage."

"I'm sorry, but that service doesn't exist. There was a trial study, but experiments on volunteers were for the most part unsuccessful. Two in one don't get on very well. A lot of malfunctions. Cases of schizophrenia, violence against the body and even suicides."

"But on your site…"

The frog bent the ends of her lips downwards, and the smile was replaced with a squeamish expression:

"Some jokers have been hacking our site and putting that advert there. My sincerest apologies. We are working on the problem." She got up. "Thank you for your interest in Human Plus. I am sorry that we have no products suitable for you at the current moment."

"Wait a second." Alisa looked the frog in the eyes. "We'd still really like to get digitised today. If we take out a mortgage on two separate bodies, what are the terms and conditions then?"

"Unfortunately, we are not currently offering implantation mortgages. Digitisation and implantation is only available for customers who are able to pay the entire sum immediately. And to those on the waiting list, of course…"

"We'd like to join the waiting list too."

"Great!" Her mouth once again stretched into a monstrous smile. "I'll put you down. It'll be your turn in… right, just a minute… in three hundred and fifty seven years."

The frog paused above the keyboard, holding that same obsequious expression.

"But we won't live that long," I said dumbly.

"Young man." The obsequiousness didn't disappear from her face, but it went stale somehow, as if it was past its sell by date. "I have an enormous waiting list for bodies. Look here." She jabbed at some endless lists on the monitor. "The majority of people on the waiting list are no longer physically alive; we have a huge archive with all their CDs which we must attend to constantly."

"So add our CDs to the database too," Alisa snapped hopelessly. "We won't do any harm."

"We have temporarily suspended the separate CD service for unpaid implantations. You can see for yourselves. Demand is significantly higher than supply."

"And how much does CD with implantation cost if you pay for it all in one go?"

The frog looked at me with something approaching pity and named a ten-digit figure. I wouldn't earn that much even in three hundred and fifty eight years.

"And is it true that some people buy several bodies at once?" Alisa asked.

"If the client has the financial wherewithal. There are no physical obstacles in this instance."

"It's not fair," Alisa sulked, looking like an eleven-year-old girl. "Some people have lots of bodies, and other people don't even have a single one."

I wanted to take her by the hand and lead her out of there.

"At the current moment you have your body. A wonderful young body." In her froggy voice you could hear both girlish envy and malicious glee.

She ran her scrutinising eyes over Alisa, as if Alisa was a dress and she was wondering whether to try it on now or later, and repeated:

"A wonderful body. I hope it will serve you for a long time to come."

"It's not fair," Alisa repeated.

The frog lost her patience:

"You know what, young lady, this is quite a strange conversation we seem to be having. What if a rich man has ten houses, and some poor man is homeless, does that mean the rich man has to give him a house?"

Alisa didn't say anything, but you could see from her face that she thought that that was indeed the best option.

"Of course he shouldn't," the woman hurriedly answered her own question. "You'd end up with some sort of communism. And we, thankfully, live in a transhumanist society."

"Transhumanism promises us victory over death," Alisa said colourlessly.

"Would you like birds?" the woman asked suddenly. "Our latest development."

"Are you making fun of us? What birds?" I asked furiously.

"Flamingos, swans, ducks, storks." Her mouth stretched into a long beneficent sliver. "Doves."

The way she said it, the word "doves" sounded somehow smutty, as if these birds were the horniest creatures on earth.

"...You could take part in an experimental programme of ours in which human CDs are implanted into the bodies of birds. In your case, two different birds, of course. All the birds listed above would suit you, as a married couple. They are monogamous, they have only one mate for several years, and some of them for their whole lives. Take doves for instance. The bird bodies retain reproductive capabilities after implantation. Which means, you understand…" She flashed her dull eyes at us, eyes full of boredom, as is often the case with Methuselahs who have already been implanted five or six times. "…the possibility of descendants. Are you, for instance," the frog fixed her murky gaze on Alisa's belly, "able to conceive?"

"I'm infertile," Alisa said quietly, but I was gripped with rage. Why discuss such private matters with a stranger who doesn't even care?

"The reason being?" the frog asked, evidently pretending she was a gynaecologist.

"No particular reason," Alisa said. "No evident pathology. Same as lots of people. Since they launched CD, women have been having children less and less. As you know full well."

"I'm infertile too," the frog confessed for some reason. "But digitisation has got nothing to do with it. It's all to do with the environment, that's what I reckon… I really do recommend you go with the doves. They're cheaper, and they're very popular, and they're ideally suited to these latitudes. A package of CD plus body implantation costs about nine hundred and seventy thousand."

"Thousand what?"

"Well not roubles, young man," the frog grinned. "You can pay in instalments. Over forty-five years."

"And how much do flamingos cost?" Alisa asked.

"One million two hundred thousand per body."

"And they'll definitely be doves, and not pigeons? I don't really like pigeons."

"Of course, young lady. Although guaranteeing doves costs seven thousand more."

"Two white doves." Alisa turned to face me. "Or two flamingos."

Her pupils were huge, like they were when we made love.

"If we pay in for forty five years, and we spend all our savings then we'll probably have enough," she said.

"I'm obliged to warn you about some of the potential drawbacks," the frog smiled. "There's only one really. The limited life span of birds with implanted human CD. About five years. After that the bird's body and the human mind will both perish. So, weigh up the pros and cons."

We said we needed to think about it, but that was a lie. Maybe the frog actually believed us, but we couldn't fool each other. We walked through the meadow and pretended that we hadn't come to any decision, but I knew that wasn't the case, and she knew it too. The image of pink birds, soaring beyond the clouds, white birds circling above the stiff, dewy corn, was too enthralling for us. Alisa and I were poisoned, beyond hope of a cure, by the anticipation of flying above that meadow.

"If we pay in for forty-five years, then we'll have enough," she said again. "And then we will fly."

"It'll be a good way to round things off," I said.

"In green pastures," Alisa said.

Never. Never now will our flights be a reality, never. Never will we tear a cloud to shreds, never know how it tastes. Never will we feel the moist trembling of the wind on the tips of our wings. Never will we see our old house from the sky, and the knots of snake-grey roads, and the meadows with their fluffy green grass, and the people, to whom we will never return. Never will we alight on stones bleached white by the sun. Never will we press together our hot white necks.

At home, that evening, we read about flamingos and doves on the net. It turned out that flamingos only lay one egg a year. And both parents feed their young with milk right from their throats. The milk is dark pink because half of it is blood. We decided that that was very beautiful and touching, but flamingos can't live in our climate and we'd have to fly far away. Plus flamingos were more expensive. And then we read that doves also feed their children milk, although it's white, with no blood. That was the last bit of convincing we needed.

"But they've got to be doves, not pigeons," Alisa said.

At dawn we wandered through the city and listened to the birds waking up. We asked ourselves: will we be able to teach ourselves to sing like that? And when we were on our way home already, I noticed that kid – the one who would later be a prosecution witness in our trial. He was walking behind us, a little way off, nodding his shaggy head along to the music coming from his headphones and impassively snapping identikit brown-grey high-rises on his smartphone. Alisa was suspicious: she believed those old wives tales about body snatchers. Who abduct people and then implant someone else's CD in them for half the price, on the black market. Then the implantees have all sorts of malfunctions, they say, and they're constantly having to go in for clean-ups, because fragments of the owner's consciousness are preserved... But this lad, he wasn't a thief, he had a very different job to do.

When we started looking at him, he nonchalantly gave us the finger and turned off into an alleyway. We forgot about him instantly.

We decided to greet the sunrise on the roof of our high-rise. We'd never gone up there before, it's forbidden. "Entering an unfenced elevated area puts at risk your body and its integrity." But that morning we just had to go out on to the roof – to see the world from a bird's eye view.

"Look how small that little guy is down there," Alisa said.

Then she went right to the very edge and held out her arms. I stood behind her and put my arms around her waist. We imagined we were one big happy bird. Two in one. That was how that little guy shot us on his smartphone – happy, on the edge of the abyss.

The charges against us were "body negligence" and "premeditated exposure of the body and its integrity to unwarranted risk", as well as some other less serious ones which I don't remember. The main pieces of evidence were the video and audio recordings of us at the entrance to Human Plus (when we had threatened to climb over the fence and hurt ourselves) and a few photographs of us standing on the edge of the roof (Alisa looks so beautiful in them!).

The witness for the defence, a neighbour from our staircase, said some high-falutin nonsense about people driven to the point of utter desperation.

On the prosecution side there were two witnesses – the guard from Human Plus, who simply confirmed that the video recording was genuine, and that teenager who had snapped us on the smartphone. The teenager had the placid, tired eyes of an old man that had been implanted many times – the type that are sometimes still called "old souls".

Before, people used to think that the soul is something like CD, just without the digitisation. That after death it could separate itself from the body and fly away – not into another body, but into the sky. I don't think I have a soul, but if I do, then I won't be flying far away. I'll stay here, on earth, as close as possible to that ancient creep pretending to be a young man. And to the guard who gave them that video recording. And to the judge who sentenced us. I'll stay here and stalk them, and poison their CDs, and appear in their dreams...

And I'll stay here so I can see my body after it's been inhabited too. And Alisa's beautiful body, Alisa's inhabited body... I'll follow them wherever they go, I'll stand behind them and whisper words in their ears without a sound, filling them with deathly sadness. I'll whisper to them that their dreams of flying will never, ever come true. Never will they tear a cloud to shreds, never will they know its taste. Never will they see their old houses and the rippling green pastures. Never will they cradle together their hot white necks. Never will they feed their children with milk, snow-white like the feathers of a dove.

The execution is tomorrow morning. They do the implantation straight after the execution, so they're going to get my body ready now for tomorrow's operation. I won't be fed at all today, but I will be given a few enemas – implantation takes place on an empty stomach, that's what the doctor told me. And actually, an empty stomach is better when it comes to the execution too. You won't be sick, you won't soil yourself, you'll go out with some dignity – that's what he said. There'll be more injections than usual today: the premeds.

Six in the evening. They ask me if I want to talk to the psychologist about my life. I don't.

Seven in the evening. The final enema.

Seven thirty in the evening. The final injection – something else along with the sedatives.

Eight in the evening. They shave my head. In its entirety. Even my eyebrows.

Eight fifteen. The psychologist comes anyway. She's a woman with an attractive, slender face and hair almost the same colour as Alisa's. But her eyes are completely different – out of large slits rimmed with black pencil stare the indifferent eyes of an "old soul". The psychologist says that, in essence, life will carry on. My mind will perish, but my body will live on. It's rather beautiful, isn't it? I ask her to leave. Obediently, she walks away.

Nine in the evening. Despite the sedatives, I can't sleep. I squat down on the floor, my eyes shut, and try not to think about anything, as if I already no longer exist. I don't know any old prayers, and transhumanist hymns make me feel sick. And so I simply repeat, again and again, the line of poetry that Alisa taught me. He maketh me to lie in green pastures. He maketh me to lie in green pastures. In green pastures…

Ten in the evening. A terrible noise outside the cell door. Loud voices, arguing. Finally, my lawyer comes in. He looks extremely happy. The appeal, he says, has been accepted, my case is going to be reviewed. Bastards, he says, they waited until the very last minute! He's as happy and excited as a little boy, he's even jumping up and down a bit on the springy cell floor. He shakes my hand and, as ever, shudders slightly when he touches the plastic on my fingers. Tomorrow morning, he says, I'll be taken out of the cell on death row and moved into an ordinary one. They'll give me some clothes, he says, and take these stupid things off my fingers. And the mouthguard off my teeth too. It's just a shame, he says, that they had time to shave your head. Oh well, it'll grow back. We'll get the sentence down, he says, to five to seven years.

"Alisa?" I ask.

Before saying that she's OK too, I spot a sort of shadow flashing across his cheerful eyes. This shadow makes his eyes look very old – but only for a fraction of a second.

When he leaves I try to feel happy – but all I feel is the urge to sleep, it pins me to the soft cell floor like a gravestone. I fall asleep quickly and clumsily — like I'm falling into a deep hole. And only in my sleep do I finally realise: the execution's been called off. I'm not falling anymore — I'm flying, flying over the city at dawn. I feel the moist trembling of the wind on the tips of my wings. I rip the cloud to shreds, it's pink, like milk from a flamingo's throat, with a slight taste of blood. I can see my prison from up in the sky, and my house, and the knots of snake-grey roads, and the windmill-shaped Human Plus building, and the meadow with the fluffy green grass… I hear a voice, which whispers:

"Will never, ever come true…"

This voice wakes me up. My heart is hammering in my throat. I get up and go to the sink. I wash my face in cold water, I wash my shaved head. The hair has already grown back a bit — the prickles of stubble feel nice on my hand. For a second I remember the feeling of the plastic tips on my fingers — body memory. It happens, it's normal. The body has its own memory that lives on for up to a year.

And these dreams — these sad, yearning, recurring dreams — the doctor says that they're normal too. That said, I've never had them before, but there's a first time for everything.

But there's no pain, nausea or tiredness. I'm in favour of a managed shut-down – it's crucial. I always ask for the sentence to be carried out in their sleep. It's like when pigs see the slaughterman in the abattoir and get scared and spoil their meat with panic: they ruin their whole body with fear during the execution — you're shattered the whole week afterwards. But when they shut them down in their sleep, without them knowing, especially after the wonderful news about the pardon, then it's completely different. It's the opposite in fact: all these endorphins, happy hormones…

This sort of execution means additional costs, of course: you've got to pay the lawyer, the prison staff etc etc – but I can afford it. And I can afford to overpay by fifty percent on each body too. The only thing is — and I'm very strict about this — selecting the bodies, all those marketing tricks, collecting evidence, photo and video recordings, legal costs — all that is paid for by the firm. Every time they try to bargain with me, but I stand firm. That said, of course, as far as professionalism is concerned, I've got no issues with the guys at Human Plus whatsoever. That bit with being implanted into birds, for instance, that was superb. You've got the perfect target audience from the get-go. Young, healthy, romantic, broke (so they're not going to hire a lawyer, just use the one they're offered), married (so no problems on the sexual side of things)...

I like taking bodies two at a time, I can afford it. Some people might think it's perverted – but if they ever got to my position socially, or even financially, I'd like to see what would happen when they get implanted into twenty bodies at once and learn how to use them in unison – then they can tell me what they think. Yes, I do like my bodies to have intercourse with each other. It's much more pleasant and more interesting than ordinary masturbation, and much more convenient than performing sex with someone external. You're both the man and the woman at the same time; you can switch focus on to the woman's body, then on to the man's and then back. You know exactly what you want, you don't have to do anything out of obligation. Plus the bodies — if they were a couple before — are a good physical match; metaphorically speaking, they remember each other.

The incident last night with the new couple was a bit disturbing, mind. Everything was going great, we were getting close to orgasm, and I switched a little bit more to the man's side (just the slightest bit so I could still feel the woman as well) and then, suddenly, at the key moment, just as it was on its way, I lost feeling in her body. I mean, it didn't seem like mine anymore. It seemed alien – a hot, wet, strange woman's body. And it got worse. For a second I almost lost the man's body too. Everything was hazy, in a sort of cloud, as if I was losing consciousness at that very moment. And then pain: these incredibly strong spasms round my solar plexus. Like there was a bird thrashing around inside me in deathly sadness. And then, I don't know why, I whispered: "Alisa" – and that pain, that yearning, left me, along with my semen, as if the bird had broken free...

Of course, I went straight to the doctor, took both bodies in for a check-up. I see the best specialist in the city, I can afford it. He's a very attentive, very experienced physician, I have every confidence in him. He questioned me for a long time – how soon after the act did sensitivity return in the bodies, how often are you bothered by bad dreams, what other symptoms do you have? I told him everything in detail.

As regards my dreams and this sense of depersonification, he said it happens: body memory lives on for up to a year. And as for the feeling that someone is following me, standing behind me – that, he said, is normal too, many implantees describe similar symptoms in the first few months after implantation: a minor conflict between the body and the new CD. It's a bit like phantom pain – the body is trying to "find" its previous owner.

But, just in case of course, he ran a test on his device to check there were no remaining fragments of someone else's consciousness. Nothing to worry about. Both bodies were all clear.

I wonder, where did I hear that poem about the "green pastures"? I've had that line in my head all day.

## SHHMOOCHIE



### 1

The story was stupid and sickly-sweet with forced positivity, and her illustrations ended up being just the same. The smugly triumphant psychologist heroine, whose speech and intellect were more reminiscent of a lobotomy victim than a highly-trained professional, would ensure nauseating happiness for her female clients – who were just as brainless and hysterical as she was – all the time imagining that she was an elf with wings. The editor had asked for particular focus on the way the elf looked: "We're going to put it on the title page." Zhenya had suggested that, instead of this, they should use the silhouette of a woman on the edge of a roof for the title page (one of the stupid women in the story was having suicidal thoughts) against the background of a sunset, or a sunrise, or some other glamorous natural phenomenon, but she was told that "in our readers' world there is no such thing as tragedy" – so she should invest all her creative energies in making the elf-psychologist.

But instead of an elf relaxing on the petals of a rose, the drawing that kept stubbornly emerging was of something fly-like, its translucent wings stuck in some bright, sticky syrup…

"The ad for Shhmoochie is on," Tasya said forlornly, looking at the TV screen. "All the girls in my class have got one, their parents bought it for them."

"And the boys?" Zhenya tried to recolour the irises and make them a touch lighter, but once more what she saw shining out from the elf's face were the compound eyes of an insect, only this time they were unnaturally blue.

"The boys too. Everyone, Mum. Everyone. Everyone's playing on them."

"And if everyone decided to jump out the window, would you jump too?" Zhenya asked dutifully, not looking up from her tablet. Her mother used to say that to her. Zhenya didn't like this shopworn, musty phrase, and she'd promised herself a hundred times that she'd stop using it, but it still slipped out, like a postprandial burp.

"I wouldn't jump," Tasya said obediently.

"Good girl," Zhenya forced herself to look up from her iPad and focus on Tasya. In her head a phrase of didactic encouragement surfaced: "Look your child in the eye as much as you can with an expression of approval and warmth." She'd read it six months back in that same magazine – back then she'd been doing some terrible illustration for them for an indecently large fee. It's not that she put much stock in the advice dished out by women's magazines – it's just that certain glossy-mag homilies had snuck into her subconscious of their own accord, like copper coins occasionally clinking away anxiously at the bottom of a piggy bank. "A warm and open look now will guarantee a trusting relationship in the future…".

"Shhmoochie: kind like a nanny," some round-faced old dear said from the screen, wearing a headscarf embroidered in gold. A dark-skinned, curly-haired boy ran up to her and she patted his head, looked him in the eye "with approval and warmth" and handed him a tablet. The shiny black case – close up – was covered in gold tracery: stardust, asteroids, comets, clusters of planets…

"That model's called Galaxy Gold," Tasya said, looking enviously at the curly-haired boy. "One of the boys in my class has got it."

("At least the design isn't completely hideous," Zhenya noted to herself.)

"Play, and feel our care," the kindly old lady, her face taking up the whole screen. Her eyes were surprisingly gentle, the colour of dark lake water. Young eyes. And her headscarf was embroidered not with flowers, but with golden planets…

"We're not going to watch adverts." Zhenya picked up the remote control but for some reason didn't turn off the TV. The curly-haired boy, there on the TV, was running his slender brown finger over the Shhmoochie's screen, and the Shhmoochie was showing him old fashioned black-and-white images. It was all sort of… cosy.

"Childhood passed as in a gentle dream," the boy said expressively, looking devotedly at the glowing screen of the Shhmoochie. "For you loved this long forsaken lad…" the glow spread over his face, giving his skin a golden hue… "Of all the Muses he remembers thee," the brown finger pressed a pink reference-cloud, and the cloud popped with an explanation:

*Alexander Pushkin, Verses dedicated to his nanny, 1821-22*

*"The Muses: in Greek mythology, poetry and literature, the Muses are the nine daughters of Zeus and Mnemosyne, who inspire literature and the arts..."*

"Right, that's enough," Zhenya snapped out of her trance and pressed the remote control; the screen went black.

"…They figure frequently in the European poetic tradition as agents of inspiration." Tasya said sadly. "The Greek word for 'muse' gives us the word museum."

"How come you know that?" Zhenya said, surprised.

"Everyone knows that. Everyone's seen that advert. But that's not enough… Please, Mummy, please," Tasya spread her arms comically wide, as if getting ready to catch an invisible ball. "Please can I have a Shhmoochie? They're really good for you. Shhmoochie: more than just a game! Play and learn…"

"Tasya, please don't talk in advertising slogans."

"OK. OK. Shhmoochie explains all the words you don't know," Tasya jabbered away. "And it's got poems too. All the ones we do at school."

"You can learn poems without any Shhmoochie."

"Not as well you can't. You don't understand, you can't learn it like you can with Shhmoochie. If you learn poems with Shhmoochie you don't forget the words."

"Rubbish."

"You don't forget the words," Tasya said with conviction. "Everyone in my class who's got a Shhmoochie gets 'A's the whole time."

"So what's on this Shhmoochie then, apart from poems?" Zhenya asked, softening a little.

"There's games too."

"What games?"

"Really good ones, interesting ones... I don't know. They don't let me play on them. They tell me: get your parents to buy you your own Shhmoochie, and leave other people's alone."

"Does Sonia Alipova say that to you too?"

"Yes."

"She's your best friend, isn't she?"

"Not any more."

"So who's your best friend now?"

"No one now." Tasya gave her a strange sort of look. "Now I'm on my own."

"Why?"

"Because they've got Shhmoochies, and I haven't. They don't hang around with that sort of person."

"What sort of person?"

Tasya didn't say anything. She looked at her very strangely. With a sort of resignation. With a gloomy certainty that the mighty have every right to destroy the world of the meek. Tasya had had that look once before... *Those little things are important*, Zhenya remembered, and immediately felt sick and ashamed. *Those tiny little things are really important, they're food for the little animals, Mummy, don't throw them away.* Two years ago she'd seen that same look on Tasya's face. In a paroxysm of domesticity, she had – for the sake of Tasya's educational development, or maybe just because she was in a bad mood – tidied up some drawers that were stuffed full of toys and drawings; at the bottom she had found little bits of dried grass, some balls of plasticine, scraps of paper, a nutshell, some plastic fragments of Kinder Surprise toys, some beads and some tiny crumbs... She threw it all away. Chucked it in a plastic bag and threw it away. And Tasya stood there and kept talking, and talking, and talking, about some nonsense or other... And only at the end, when the bag was already stuffed full and all tied up, did it dawn on her. The dried crumbs were food for stuffed animals, the crumpled sweet wrapper was a little bed for a rubber mouse, the dry leaf was a present from a friendly tree, the beads were precious gems, and the chunk of polystyrene was magical... She threw it away, that plastic bag. It was too late to give in. It would be harmful, for her emotional development. That was the first time she'd seen that look. Not angry, not hurt. The disappointment of a tiny little animal that finds that its burrow has been destroyed...

"...Are they mean to you? In school?"

"No."

"Are you telling the truth?"

"Yes."

"So they're not mean to you?"

"No, they're not." Tasya thought for a second. "They just don't notice me."

## 2

You can purchase **Shhmoochie** at any
Nannyland sales centre 24 hours a day.
Bring your kids! Before purchase they'll take a fun and exciting quiz!
Using the results of the test, Nannyland experts can select the individual
**Shhmoochie** console that best suits your offspring!
**Shhmoochie** is the answer to all your problems: bring happiness home!

**Shhmoochie**. More than just a game. Play and learn.

* Contingent on the results of the free test,
orphan children will be given consoles free of charge.

Painted-on logs quietly crackled in the electric hearth, and the sound of this crackling occasionally sent a tickly shiver running across Zhenya's skin. Multi-coloured Shhmoochies shimmered behind the glass in towering wall-length cabinets like extraterrestrial Christmas tree decorations. Zhenya looked at them and tried to imagine what this strange, unearthly tree would look like all decked out – but for some reason instead of a tree she imagined the branching silvery pattern of a computer microcircuit. The Shhmoochies made her eyes swim.

Zhenya squinted and leant back on the velvety, smoky-purple back of the sofa in expectation of another wave of shivers. The wave came, sweeping from the back of her head to her cheeks, and it felt nice. And there was a nice smell – it was stronger when she closed her eyes. Nannyland smelled of libraries and Christmastime – not Christmas these days, all fake and plastic like a cheap Chinese toy, but the real one, from her childhood. The smell of bitter chocolate, satsuma peel and wilting pine needles mixed with the spicy scent of well-thumbed pages. There weren't any old books, pine trees or satsumas in Nannyland, but the smell was there, the rich, perfect smell of a child's happiness. It seemed to envelope you in an instant, to gently pat your head, to protect you from harm... Everything here was velvety, purple and smoky, like kitten fur. Like dandelion seedballs ... seedballs made from smoky fur... scraps of fur, shot through with static, flying into the sky in a perfect geometrical wedge...

"Can't wait, can you, poppet? This is our cabinet, and, look, here's our shelf!"

Zhenya woke from her comfy dozing when Tasya and the sales-girl came back from the playroom. She pressed a button to reanimate the extinguished asphalt-grey screen of her mobile: one new message, from her editor – "so where is it?"; time – 23:30. Tasya's been gone a whole hour – and she'd been asleep the whole time... They shouldn't have come here so late! It was such a childish thing to do: just to check if they really were open 24/7. Now her daughter won't get enough sleep.

"Mummy, I won, I won!" She thrust a drawing in Zhenya's face. "And look at the drawing we did!"

"Who's 'we'?" Zhenya glanced quickly at a drawing of a princess with golden curls.

"Well, me. They had a free Shhmoochie drawing lesson, they showed me how to draw and I drew it, with colouring pencils, they let me use colouring pencils..."

"Your offspring has a real talent," the sales-girl said sweetly, "for creating images. The test was a success. You may purchase a Shhmoochie."

"And if the test hadn't been a success, then, of course, you wouldn't sell us Shhmoochie for any money," Zhenya shot back with no real malice.

"We would not sell it," the girl said seriously. "For any money."

She was wearing a headscarf with golden planets on it, like the one in the TV ad. When Zhenya looked at her in surprise she quickly pulled out a smile, but her eyes weren't laughing.

"OK, I see," Zhenya said. "Marketing. As if Shhmoochie is only for the chosen few."

"On the contrary. Such incidents are extremely rare," said the sales-girl.

"What 'incidents'?"

"A child being unable to pass the test."

"Mummy, did I get it right when I said 'travelling' for the question about Daddy? The other answers were 'Daddy is dead' and 'Daddy doesn't live with us', but our Daddy does live with us, he's just gone away, right?"

"Was there no 'Daddy got abducted by aliens' option?" Zhenya asked darkly. "What are you doing asking a child questions like that? It's not as if we've come to a psychologist."

"There wasn't an aliens option," Tasya said seriously. "So was 'travelling' right or not?"

Tasya had that look on her face again – the one she always had when asking about her father – as if she'd been presented with a box covered in wrapping paper and bows and she was trying to guess what the present was hiding inside. And, as ever, Zhenya couldn't summon the strength to tell her the truth, to steal that present away:

"You got it right, Tasya."

"The questions and exercises in our fun little test are compiled by psychologists," the sales-girl chimed in. "They help us get inside the child's inner world and determine exactly which games console is most psychologically suitable for your offspring... Come on, sweet-pea," she turned to Tasya. "Which one do you fancy? What a good girl. You passed our test!"

Doing a little jig of excitement, Tasya stared lovingly at the Shhmoochies on display behind the glass.

Offspring. Sweet-pea. Thank God it's not "kiddywink". Where does this folksy tone comes from? And these headscarves they wear. And the name of the company – Nannyland... Maybe they're Slavic nationalists? And what kind of weird rules are these – you have to pass a test? What if the child is, say, autistic?

"And what if your offspring is, say, autistic?" she said out loud. "What then? Would you sell them this thing then? Or if they're disabled in some other way? Mentally deficient..." she didn't like the way that sounded. "I mean, mentally... unusually..."

"Alternatively gifted," the sales-girl suggested with a smile.

"Exactly. So if an alternatively gifted child doesn't pass this test of yours, do they not get a Shhmoochie? So you end up with a sort of eugenics?"

"We appreciate your concern," the girl purred. "I can assure you: there's nothing to worry about. Autistic and other alternatively gifted children always do well in the test... What's the matter, are you lost, poppet?" she switched her attention to Tasya. "Here, from this shelf, you deserve something from this shelf."

Tasya looked warily at her mother – on the shelf she'd "deserved" stood the gleaming Shhmoochies from the Fairy Rosie range: different shades of pink and pearl packaging, with sparkly gold flecks and fairy-tale illustrations.

"I like this one," Tasya said, pointing at a glittering mid-pink Shhmoochie, then immediately asked Zhenya in a terrified whisper: "Is it tacky?"

There was hope in Tasya's eyes: maybe this time it won't be. She had a difficult relationship with pink, sparkles, princesses and so on. Thanks to Zhenya's efforts she knew that things like that were vulgar trash, but in her heart of hearts she still loved all and them, and the short, harsh word "tacky" sounded more pitiful than offensive when she said it. And now she's being offered, legitimately it seems, something amazing, something beautiful and unabashedly pink, with fairies, trolls and princes on it. And it's blatantly obvious that it's tacky.

"Aha, sooo this is the Shhmoochie that's caught your eye! Such a pretty one!" the sales-girl sang out like a siren. "A fantastic choice! This model is called 'The Magic Castle', it's completely..."

"We'd be better off choosing from that case over there, with the planets," Zhenya stopped her short. "The Galaxy Golds."

"Unfortunately, that's not possible," the siren said. "According to the results of her test, your child can choose her Shhmoochie only from the Fairy Rosie range."

"But we don't like Fairy Rosie!" Zhenya said angrily.

"Your daughter does."

"Nothing of the sort! It was you who told her to pick from that shelf! And to draw some idiotic Barbie princess! I'm not going to buy my daughter some pink sequin trash just because you're having trouble shifting them! You can rip someone else off, thank you very much. I'm trying to help my daughter develop good taste. You like those ones, the ones with the planets, don't you Tasya?"

Tasya looked silently over at the Galaxy Golds and lowered her eyes. She turned the drawing round to face her and squeezed it to her chest. The siren gave Zhenya a conciliatory smile.

"We appreciate your concern. Don't worry, the questions and exercises in our fun test are compiled in such a way that they allow us to determine exactly which games console is most aesthetically suitable for your offspring." The siren opened the Fairy Rosie cabinet with a little gold key. "In this case that's the Magic Castle Shhmoochie in the Fairy Rosie range." She took the tablet down from the shelf. "That'll be three thousand, four hundred and ninety nine roubles."

"Fantastic," Zhenya hissed. "So we get to pay but we don't get to choose?"

"You have chosen," the girl said. Her voice was simultaneously both sweet and harsh, like rancid Turkish delight.

"We'll go to a different shop."

"By all means, if that's more convenient for you. But we have a unified database, and this is the only model you will be offered in any other shop."

"Right, we're going." Zhenya took Tasya by the hand; the drawing fell and rustled on the floor. The girl dashed to pick it up.

Her hand was hot, damp and sort of floppy, like the paw of a soft toy that's been ruined in the washing machine.

"Mummy, please," Tasya whined. "Please, Mummy, please, let's get a Rosie, please..." Her chin started wobbling. "Let's get a Rosie here..."

Tasya's cheeks were red, with an uneven pale border around them, and curls of her hair stuck to her temples. Zhenya leaned over and touched her forehead with her lips. Roasting.

"Do you take cards?"

"Yes, of course, we take Visa... Don't cry, don't be upset, sweet-pea," the girl cooed, handing Tasya her drawing. "Mummy's going to buy you a Shhmoochie now. Would you like that wrapped?"

3

Hey there!
My name's Fairy Rosie – what's yours?
Oh, what a beautiful name!
I've wanted to be your friend for so long!
Now I've got you and you've got me.
I promise you: you're never going to be alone again.
Do you want me to tell you a secret?
Just make sure no one is spying on us.
Go into your room and don't forget to shut the door.
My programme is made especially for you.
And not for anyone else.

**Shhmoochie**: more than just a game. Always by your side.

Sonia Alipova's hyperactive mother caught up with her in the school cloakroom:

"Yevgenia, while you were ill you missed the collection for the photo album!" Since the beginning of the school year, the mothers had established this tradition of calling each other by their full names, but without surnames. "Yesterday was the final day. But I paid for you."

"Thanks, um, er..." Zhenya realised that she couldn't remember the woman's name. "... How much do I owe you?"

"That'll be a thousand roubles, Yevgenia."

The proposed sum for some reason alerted the part of her brain responsible for Biblical names. 'Maria' unexpectedly popped into her head.

"A thousand roubles." Zhenya pulled out the only note in her purse. "Maria, so this photo album, it's made of gold, is it?"

"No, it's more sort of silvery," Maria flapped. "And there's this fruit along the edges, apples, cherries, all different berries, branches and bluebells, and they all intertwine, in this, you know, border, and in the middle there's this little oval, and in it…" Maria held a beatific pause "… a photo of your Totsie."

"Tasya."

"I know, Yevgenia, I know, of course! That's just my pet name for her! Totsie, Tottikins, Totteroo, that's just what I call little kiddies! Right, I'll tick you off as having paid!"

Maria giggled, covering her mouth with a trembling, chubby, beringed hand, then pulled a notebook from her shiny bag, scribbled something inside and then scanned the cloakroom with a deranged look. Little kids had an effect on her like amphetamines, they stimulated her nervous system.

"Yevgenia, I saw you've finally bought your little daughter a Shhmoochie!" Mrs Sukhodolskaya, a mother with a whole brood of kids, joined the conversation. "I'm so happy for you!" She grabbed Zhenya's hand and shook it. "Now everything's going to be OK! Everything's going to be OK!"

Normally feeble and exhausted, Sukhodolskaya was now in some sort of state of sickly, feverish excitement. A half-dried-out crown of dandelions sat skewiff on her head.

"You've got a Fairy Rosie, I think?" she asked, for some reason switching to a whisper.

"Magic Castle," Zhenya confirmed.

"Wonderful! My eldest has got a Fairy too, but Magic Garden. One of the boys has a Galaxy Gold and the other one's got a Star Battle."

"We've got a Pretty Kitty," Maria said. "We're thrilled, Yevgenia, that you've bought your Totsie a Shhmoochie. But why did you wait so long? We were starting to think you were rejects."

"What?"

"You know, rejects. Who couldn't pass the test. Who aren't sold a Shhmoochie."

"There's one of them in this school." Sukhodolskaya leaned into Zhenya's ear. "In 2b. Vinogradov."

Sukhodolskaya gave off a sour smell of wilted grass and stale sweat, like a cow. Zhenya moved back politely. Then she asked: "So what, he's different somehow?"

"A difficult child," Maria said evasively.

Zhenya had seen Vinogradov a couple of times, during break time. Both times, he'd been squatting down with his back pressed against the fence. His classmates were chucking grey grit from the sandpit at him. He was fat and wore an emerald green baseball cap. The teacher on duty pretended he hadn't seen it. Zhenya also pretended she hadn't seen it.

"...He's retarded." Sukhodolskaya breathed in Zhenya's face again.

"You can't say that!" Zhenya objected. "If you, an adult, go round giving a boy a label like that, then the children are going to repeat it!" She even raised her voice; it suddenly seemed incredibly important to put Sukhodolskaya to shame, as if with this speech she could make amends for the fact that she hadn't intervened when he was being bullied back then in the school playground.

## 4

**Shhmoochie.**

Scared of the dark? Not any more. Play and forget your fears.
Play and have sweet dreams.

This product cannot be exchanged or returned.

While she was walking Tasya back from school, when they were almost home, on Komsomolsky Prospekt, she saw him again. In her peripheral vision. From behind. A blue T-shirt – the one he was wearing when he had gone out back then, a T-shirt like a million others in this town. Black hair sticking up on the back of his head – every third guy has hair like that. A cigarette in his left hand – there's no shortage of left-handed smokers around. And the way he walked – slightly pigeon-toed, sort of adorable, he would always wear out the inside of his shoes first. For a long time she didn't throw them out, she was waiting – he had left his things, that means he's coming back... No, he didn't come back. All he would do is flash by occasionally – like a coward, from behind, in the distance, on the half-turn, in a crowd, on the metro, in underpasses, behind train doors slamming shut, on the far side of panes of murky municipal glass – he would flash by and then hide. This time he dived into an underpass on the far side of Komsomolsky Prospekt and didn't reappear.

Four years had passed and he would still appear to her – a slouching, mocking ghost. Other men, men who leave properly – with rowing and swearing, with insults, tears and curses – other men would probably not carry on appearing in distant hallucinations, on staircases leading underground. Other men leave for some young dolly bird with no kids, or raise some other woman's difficult teenage son, or they go and rent a flat in some sleepy suburb, or they take their mum to Israel, or turn to drink, or get into an accident, or they die in hospital.

Other men – yes, but Danila left in such a mundane, improbable, improvised way, it was like he'd never left at all. One Saturday evening he had headed out to the supermarket for some cigarettes, some Chilean red, cherry tomatoes and a Kinder Surprise for Tasya – and he hadn't come back. He never came back.

It had taken roughly two years to accept this "never". In the meantime she had been weaving a spider's web in a dark corner of her mind – and he thrashed about in it like a fly, caught alive in the sticky, intertwining mesh of her hopes, hurts and hypotheses. Then he went quiet and dried out – but he would still come back to life occasionally and tug painfully at the threads.

Men don't leave like that – the table laid, promising chocolate and tomatoes. They don't leave like that – deserting a three-year-old daughter and a young wife they've screwed an hour earlier. Not giving her time for suspicions or hysterics. Not giving her a chance to curse him, or at least lament him – not before he left and not after.

She would have taken him for dead – smeared over the tarmac by a truck, torn to pieces by thugs in an alleyway, falling in the springtime mud gripping his heart... She would have taken him for an "unidentified corpse", lost in some morgue somewhere, which she, of course, had called (she'd called them all), but the sleepy women hadn't wanted to cut short their tea break, those sleepy women stirring their teas maniacally with little spoons and saying "We haven't had anyone like that in", but, but... But people don't die like that either. He took too much money with him, a lot more than he needed for cigarettes and tomatoes, and he took his passport too. At work they said he'd asked for his record of service card the day before (he hadn't taken it, incidentally). And a week later his Facebook page was "deleted by user". And his mother, who lives in Podolsk, said that he'd just come to visit her and had left only an hour ago – but she's got dementia, she could've got him confused with someone else or got the year wrong... And some time later certain kind-hearted people would inform her that they'd seen him in Tallinn or in Riga, with some ugly flaxen-haired local woman, but, maybe, of course, he wasn't with that woman, and maybe it wasn't even him, just someone who looked a lot like him…

Disappeared without trace. A lot of people have disappeared without trace in Russia, a whole army. Sometimes Zhenya would imagine a long, bloody, fiery war hidden from the world that this whole army has been sent to. It was a good image, fitting – her husband away at war. He could easily be killed there or has even already been killed. She preferred to think of him as dead.

You could love a dead man, miss him, cherish his memory. Alive he was a piece of shit and a traitor that she needed to forget for good.

Tasya immediately went to go and play with her Fairy Rosie, and shut the door. She had acquired this habit when she was sick – shutting herself in her room. Previously, by contrast, she couldn't stand closed spaces and used to ask Zhenya to leave a crack in the door at night; Zhenya was even worried that Tasya might have claustrophobia. But now – not a problem. She shut the door quietly, politely – but firmly, with no cracks. Zhenya tried to talk to her about it for a bit, along the lines of: don't shut yourself up in your room playing with your Shhmoochie non-stop, people only close the door when they want to hide something and what secrets could you have from your own mummy…? "What secrets, Mummy?" she looked at her like she was ill. "It's just so I don't get in your way. Because you're working."

And it was true – she didn't get in the way now. She didn't tug at her, she didn't ask questions, she didn't ask her to read her stories, she didn't turn on cartoons at full volume on her computer, she didn't demand that Zhenya come and watch her dolls and animals drinking invisible tea from a toy tea-service.

Rosie answered all her questions and Rosie read her stories – a throaty, cosy, quiet mechanical voice would seep through Tasya's closed door, reading out poems from the school syllabus and some others which Zhenya either didn't know or couldn't recognise from the fragments that reached her. It didn't irritate Zhenya, that voice; on the contrary, it wrapped around her, as if she was being swaddled in her grandmother's blanket, and under this blanket she could work easily and quietly, and her drawings were playful and a little naïve, and the editor liked them and called them "touching".

Tasya barely played with her dolls at all now, she said it was boring, that it was way more interesting to play with her Shhmoochie. "Show me these games," Zhenya had asked her once. "Just not now, later, right now I'm working, show me later." But later, of course, they forgot about it; that is, Tasya forgot about it, Zhenya remembered, theoretically, but she really did have a lot of work on – a new commission, a sequel to the story of the stupid psychologist lady – and she had no interest in messing about with a games console, although she knew, of course, that you have to keep an eye on what games your child is playing. And she knew that it wasn't right actually: your child is sitting there, deep in her Shhmoochie, for days on end, and even falls asleep with that tablet, literally hugging it, as she used to with her fox teddy... But Tasya really did keep out of her way, and she had so much work on. It's just for a while. Just a couple of weeks, that's it, then she'll definitely spend some time with her. But for now – it was as if she'd hired Tasya a nanny. After all, that's how they advertise these consoles: "Shhmoochie – the console that's as kind as a nanny. Play and feel our care..."

"...Night night, Mum!"

She hadn't even noticed Tasya going to bed.

"Have you washed?" she yelled through the door.

"Yes!"

"Washed your hands?"

"And brushed your teeth?"

"Yes!" Tasya said triumphantly. "My Shhmoochie always reminds me!"

"OK, I'll come in and say good night in a minute."

"Maybe... you don't have to?" Tasya's voice sounded stressed.

"Have to what?" Zhenya didn't understand.

"To come in. We can say good night like this."

Zhenya was so surprised that she shut her laptop without saving changes.

"What do you mean I don't have to?" Her own voice seemed shrill and stupid, like a clucking chicken. She leapt up, she wanted to go in and see Tasya. Shut. It was shut from the inside somehow, although there's no lock there.

"Tasya, sweetie!" Once again a sort of clucking noise came out. "What, don't you want to kiss your mummy good night? Why have you locked yourself away in there?" She pulled at the handle, and changed her tone. "What right do you have to lock yourself in? Who gave you permission?"

"I haven't locked myself in," Tasya whinged, insulted. "The door's just stiff."

Zhenya gave it a forceful shove with her shoulder. It really just was stiff and it opened.

She went over to Tasya, leaned over her and talked to her in a cutesy little voice, as if she was three years old:

"What's the matter, baby, has Mummy upset her little baby? Why doesn't my little baby want to say good night to me?"

"I'm not a baby," Tasya said seriously. "And you haven't upset me. It's just... I didn't want you to see my room. You'll say it's tacky."

Zhenya looked around. The walls in the room were covered in smooth, goldish material with sparkly flecks in it, right on top of the wallpaper. It was something like satin – she ran her hand over it – yes, it's silky to the touch. But no, where could Tasya have got this much silk from? It's just synthetic. Of course it's synthetic. But where had she got it from…? Tasya had stuck bits of pink ribbon, wound into spirals, to the tulle curtains, like flower buds. On the table there was a dish, a crystal one, from a dinner service that had long since been buried in a box in the loft space (had she got up into the loft space *by herself*? Had she dug through all the junk in there *by herself*? She'd probably found that gold cloth there too, there's all sorts of rubbish up there, that loft space has been needing a clean-out for ages); in the dish there was some water, and in the water, trembling slightly, were round scented candles in aluminium holders and some rose petals. The height of vulgarity, Nabokov would have called it, an imitation of beauty. A child's right to creative freedom, the magazine Zhenya was working for would say, to self-expression and imagination, don't impose limits, encourage them. Yes, encourage her. After all, she has tried, she's done it all very neatly and, in places, with a bit of talent. Stylishly even. It's kitsch, of course, but why not. Praise your child. Otherwise your child will become distant.

"How lovely," Zhenya said, "Have you made a room for a princess?"

Hanging on the wall above her bed, pinned to the gold satin, was Tasya's drawing – the one which she had done at the test. A yellow-haired, green-eyed princess wearing a crown. Around the edge of the piece of paper was a "wooden" frame drawn in pencil. Not, actually, a bad portrait. Quite good actually. In pencil, although Tasya usually used felt-tip pens. There's some symmetry. Horizontal and vertical axes… All the proportions are there. But there's also that slight inaccuracy, too, that gives the face a certain expressiveness. And the eyes… It's amazing that a seven-year-old child can draw such lifelike eyes. The upper eyelid is covering the iris slightly, with a soft shadow underneath it. And just the right distance between the lower lid and the iris. And two bright lines, made with a rubber, running from the corners to the pupil – the "wet eye" effect. And even the flash of light stuck to the left of the pupil, showing the reflection of something… a window?

"It's a room for a fairy," Tasya said. "The fairy's quarters in the magic castle. And the portrait is of a fairy, not a princess."

"She's very beautiful. You've done a good job, it's a very good drawing."

"But I already showed you that drawing. You said it was tacky."

"I was wrong." Zhenya stroked Tasya's hair.

"Really?"

"Really. It's not tacky."

Tasya relaxed – even her hair seemed softer, more pliant. Golden tresses…

"Now I'm even better at drawing," Tasya gabbled. "Because there's this program on my Shhmoochie, Paintlife, it teaches you to paint, and I've got to the second level already, I really like the lessons, I can paint a person, and a horse, and still lives, and bouquets..."

She felt ashamed – tiny little needles jabbed her eyes and throat. A games console was teaching her daughter to draw. Not her, a professional artist, but this program, Paintlife. How could she have let this happen? How could she have abandoned her little girl?

She wanted to fix everything, to make amends, to sort things out, right now, straight away, to make everything better, as soon as possible. When was the last time she'd sung her daughter a bedtime song? A year ago? A year and a half? Fix everything. They had their favourite song. She smoothed Tasya's hair and remembered the words in dribs and drabs. About the lamb. Mary and the little lamb. A nice song...

"Mary had a little lamb, little lamb, little lamb," Zhenya started crooning. "And his fleece was white as snow, And everywhere that Mary went, Mary went, Mary went..."

"Mummy, I don't want that song."

"It's our favourite, isn't it?"

"I don't like it anymore."

Don't take offence. It's not her daughter's fault. It's *her* fault...

"Which one do you like?"

"The one about the fairies."

"I don't know the one about the fairies."

"Don't worry, Shhmoochie will sing it to me. I've got it here in Lullabies..." Tasya drew her slender finger over the screen. "I listen to it at bedtime."

"Can I listen to it with you?" Zhenya asked.

"If you like you can listen to the first verse," Tasya tucked the tablet under her pillow and closed her eyes.

Don't take offence. Listen. Give her a kiss and then leave quietly.

"The five fairies," Shhmoochie cooed sweetly from under the pillow.

Pipes started playing, a violin joined in, then a woman's voice, crystalline and trembling with tenderness:

*Each fairy will hug her sisters and go*
*Together to make a bonfire glow*
*Together their food in a pot they'll seethe*
*Together the garden flowers weave*
*And into the pond together they'll dive.*

Zhenya kissed Tasya on the top of her head and quietly left the room. A strange song. It was as if it didn't start at the beginning.

"Close the door, please," Tasya said sleepily.

## 5

Thank you Nannyland.

**Shhmoochie**: giving everyone the gift of happiness

"Mariana tore her hands from her face and took some hasty gulps of water. Tears ran down her cheeks.

'That rat,' she said, her eyes flashing with passion. 'You have no idea how much I hate him!'

'I know, I know,' Nadia said calmly; once again she felt the thin, transparent wings twitching beneath her silk blouse. 'Please, calm down. I'm here to help you.'

She looked at the weeping Mariana with an expression that was at once firm and wise..."

"Screw you," Zhenya said to the unfinished elf-psychologist.

There were no eyes. That is, there was an overall outline, grey ovals with little circles inside – like coins in the eye-sockets of a corpse. Bloody computer, it hadn't saved the latest changes for some reason. The right eye had been all done, and the left one had just needed a few finishing touches. Now she had to do it all again from scratch. Right. We're going to have a green iris, emerald-green... Not piercing, but muted, blurred, like the glass of a broken bottle licked smooth by the waves. The endless waves, one following another...

"*He followed her to school one day, school one day, school one day,*" Zhenya started humming, to make work a bit more fun.

...The upper lid covers the iris a bit, like so... And a soft shadow underneath... *Which was against the rules*... Just the right distance between the lower lid and the iris... *It made the children laugh and play*... And now we make two bright lines, from the corners to the pupil, the "wet eye" effect ... *It made the children laugh and play*... A slightly babyish technique, but the editor will like it... *Laugh and play, laugh and play*... We stick a flash of light to the pupil, on the left, which reflects – what should it reflect? The office window. Or no, maybe that stupid Mariana instead. The one that "tears her hands from her face". Zhenya giggled. She imagined hands pulled from cheeks, covered in flesh.

"'...That's your anger talking, Mariana.' Nadia subtly switched to her patient's first name to create an atmosphere of trust. 'Kill your anger, calm your pride, forgive your man.'

'Forgive him? That scumbag?!'

'Forgive him, forgive him,' Nadia nodded with a kind smile and beneath her blouse her wings started to flutter. 'Accept him as he is. Don't ask too many questions, they'll scare him away.'

'But then I'll never figure out who it was he slept with?'

'So much the better.' Nadia touched Mariana's hand. 'So much the better, my dear...'"

She saved the changes and wanted to close the file – but something held her back, some invisible splinter. As if she'd forgotten something. Something important, something obvious. You're being neurotic, Zhenya told herself, continuing to grope through her thoughts and memory looking for this strange splinter. Just being neurotic. Nadia the psychologist would have said it was because she was underfucked. Not in so many words of course: "You are not getting enough love and affection."

"Yep, not nearly enough." She looked up at Nadia's bottle-green eyes on the monitor – and suddenly she realised. She fingered the splinter lodged in her mind and gave it a tweak.

This drawing of Nadia, this elf-psychologist – she'd stolen it. Not just now, but two weeks back, when she had done the illustrations for the first story – she'd stolen the face, the whole image. Stolen them from Tasya. From the very drawing she'd done in the test, the one now hanging in her room. Just in case, she went into her Sent folder and checked the dates – yes, there it was. She had sent the editor the drawing the morning of the 22nd. And she and Tasya had gone to Nannyland on the evening of the 21st. Then they'd gone home, Tasya had had a temperature up around 40, she was babbling something incoherent, crying, jabbing at the picture, and Zhenya had given her something to bring her temperature down, got her into bed somehow, running back every five minutes to check her forehead while the editor was inundating her with emails and texts – "so where is it?", "when?!", "we're going to miss the deadline", "oh God!" – and she had done the drawing – in bursts, by intuition, in a hurry – and at half-five in the morning, she'd sent it... "Thanks, it's very touching!"

She attached the picture to the email and pressed "Send". It's looks similar – so what. Someday Tasya and she will laugh about this. Right now it's time for a shower. She liked to take a shower whenever she finished a drawing. As if she was washing off the greasy marks of paint and the smell, as she used to – although now her hi-tech job left neither marks nor smells, just fatigue and a feeling as if she had dry glass dust in her eyes.

"Mary had a little lamb…"

It had got stuck in her head… The streams of water tickled her breasts and stomach; she made it warmer. Her still beautiful breasts. Still perky, not drooping, but no one wanted them… She rubbed her nipples, and they shrank, obedient and trusting, taking it for a caress, remembering the touch of a man's fingers, confusing her own body with someone else's. It's amazing how easy it is to trick your breasts and your clitoris. Zhenya squeezed a little puddle of honey-milk slime from the tube, spread it over her stomach and breasts, slipped the middle finger of her right hand in, parted the smooth folds in the thick wiry scrub, felt the warm slippery pearl in the midst of the oyster flesh… It was Danila who had come up with the comparison with the oyster and the pearl. He used to say that *down there* she smelled of the sea and of salty seaweed… *Everywhere that Mary went*… No, not a pearl, a pearl is dead, just a grain of sand, wrapped in calcium carbonate; no, she's got something else – she's got a small, living, throbbing muscle, it controls her movements, her pulse, it opens and closes those soft folds, it throws her open, cracks her open like an overripe shell.

A sound. Strange, out of place, alarming. She turned off the water and froze in a prickly mist of instantly cooling droplets. The sound of a metal wand carefully poking around in the lock. In her lock. No one has a key to their house. There's no one who could be coming in right now… Her heart is beating, stronger and faster, like a pendulum swinging on the other side of her ribs on a cold thin chain… Crunch-crunch. The joints in the door lock crack… The chain breaks and falls, her heart leaps into her throat, rolls right up to her chin and gets stuck there, convulsing jerkily. For a second, it's quiet. Then the sound of the front door opening. Slam – it's closed. Quiet again. Steps. Rustling. Oh God, Tasya's out there.

She pulled back the curtain and climbed out, wet and naked, on to the icy tiles. Choking on the living lump stuck in her throat, she grabbed some nail scissors in her trembling fingers, the only "weapon" she had in the bathroom; she dropped them in the sink, she grabbed them again; all the while calm and detached, like a disinterested observer, she noticed that she wound herself in a terrycloth towel and checked her hair in the mirror before going out to face whoever had invaded her home, as if she wanted to observe all the proper niceties…

"Hi," Danila said. "I thought you'd be asleep already, so I didn't ring the doorbell. I've got a key after all."

For some reason he proffered the key, holding it out on his upturned palm like a precious gem. As if it was the Golden Key from the story of Pinocchio and wasn't just the key to the door, but the key to their whole life together. As if this key explained four years of confusion, yearning and fatigue.

The terrycloth towel fell off. He smiled, at once guilty and shameless, not looking away. She stood there, dumb, numb all over, naked, wet, gripping the nail scissors in her whitened fingers, and he looked her up and down, as if she was a mollusc plucked from its shell.

"You're so beautiful."

She picked up the towel and covered herself, all the time pointing those stupid scissors at him.

"I bought some wine." He indicated the bag on the floor. "And tomatoes. And a Kinder Surprise for Tasya." He furrowed his brow in concern. "She still likes Kinder Surprise doesn't she?"

"Kinder Surprise," Zhenya said again and for some reason suddenly started giggling. "Kinder. Surprise."

She was laughing, literally shaking with laughter, but the dispassionate and attentive observer in her noticed that breaking through the laughter were hiccups and sobs, that tears were pouring from her eyes and hanging ticklishly on her chin, and that he had carefully taken the scissors off her, and that he had embraced her.

"Forgive me," he whispered, touching her ear with his lips.

*forgive your man*

"...Don't kick me out, I'm begging you. I can't live without you. Without you both. Please let me stay."

She wanted to say, get out, you managed to live without us this long. She wanted to say: I hate you. To say: you shithead. But

*that's your anger talking*

she really did want to let him stay, to not kick him out. For him to squeeze her, to beg her, to breathe in her ear those hot words that she had dreamed of hearing for so many years.

She wanted to ask: where have you been, who have you been with, how dare you, but

*accept him as he is, don't ask too many questions*

she decided that she'd ask later. Some other time.

They stood there, embracing, and his T-shirt soaked up moisture from her towel. That same T-shirt he had been wearing when he left.

"What, you've been wearing that T-shirt non-stop for four years?"

"No, I bought myself new ones. But I kept this one to remind me of home. I missed you so much."

*So why didn't you just come home?!*

*don't ask too many questions*

"It's so good to be home."

Tasya came out of the nursery, shaggy-haired and squinting in the light. She recognised him and started jumping up and down:

"Daddy!"

It was as if the box with the present in it, hidden from her for so long, had at last been opened.

## 6

For any children unable to pass our fun little test,
Nannyland provides consolation prizes.

On Saturday afternoon they went, as a family, to Interiors, a shop on the Frunzenskaya Embankment and bought the three tins of paint they needed, and it was magical. Life is like this sometimes. As if you've been wrapped in a thin, transparent film of happiness, and you're like a ripe exotic fruit in an expensive supermarket, this film covers you entirely – eyes and ears, and nostrils, and skin, and mucous membranes; and everything you look at through this film is exquisite; and everything you touch through it is gold.

Everything was magical, absolutely everything: the embankment itself, with its back-combed coat of poplar fluff; the long-legged, muscly women gliding through this fluff, looking like thoroughbred horses shackled in the metal and plastic of rollerblades; the old biddy tracking them with a thoughtful gaze, with cheerful wrinkles around her eyes and in the corners of her mouth, with a bag of stale odds and ends of bread for the birds; even the pigeons surrounding the old woman, stupid and excited, like a mob of football fans, but still birds, still wild and bold, still capable of launching themselves off the trampled asphalt, away from the spit, the fag ends and the stale crumbs, and soaring up into the eternal vacant cold of the heavens; and all these luxury interior design shops along the embankment, with their burgundy curtains, gigantic chandeliers, bronze statues, cubic beds and granite chairs, their overloaded window displays staring proprietorially at the river in its stone housing and at the glass bridge that looks like an expensive conservatory, as if the river and the bridge were just a continuation of their range of designer goods.

Not long ago Zhenya had neither understood nor liked all these crazy expensive objects. A gilded chandelier the size of a human being – who needs that? Who would want something like that, even for free, still less for seven thousand euros? Now she understood: in an ordinary, boring, grey apartment a chandelier like that would be ridiculous, but in their castle – they were doing their place up to look like a castle – it would fit perfectly. It's a pity they didn't have a spare seven thousand euros lying around. She's just saying that, actually. In fact she has no complaints and no desires because she has plenty enough already. It was like an enormous puzzle which she had been trying to finish for years – a puzzle that just refused to form a complete, intelligible picture, that had remained hopelessly fragmentary: since Danila had come back it's not as if it had all come together in its entirety, but it had finally revealed to her, in broad terms, the main theme of her life story, its essential, key elements. Now it was all there. There was Danila and there was Tasya, and they were doing up the flat, and at Tasya's request they were turning the flat into a castle, and all of them were painting all the walls and ceilings together, and they didn't have enough Medieval Red Wine, and it was summer and they had gone to the shop and bought the tins they needed and it was marvellous. Life can be like that sometimes. Like you've been impregnated with happiness, and now you're just quietly incubating it, and everything, absolutely everything around you, is nourishment for your foetus…

…They'd just turned into 1st Frunzenskaya Street when the wind carried the sound of children's shouts from the river and threw it at their backs – happy and penetrating like the cries of gulls over the sea. Zhenya stopped and turned to face the voices, involuntarily preparing a smile, expecting to receive yet another everyday miracle for the piggy bank of everyday miracles she'd collected that day. Children playing by the riverside – they're probably throwing bread to the ducks or maybe waving at the boats as they sail by – how lovely, how… What?

They were not playing.

Her first instinctive desire was to turn back and keep going with her family, to just go home. As if nothing was happening down there by the river. They're probably just messing around. She turned back, but the little scene she had managed to see did not fit with the day's succession of happy events, like a disproportionately long shadow in a picture of a cloudless noon. She had to fix the picture, to get rid of the defect.

"Daniiiila," she sang out imploringly. "Do you think you could go and quickly take a look at what's going on down there?"

He looked at the river:

"Look at what? It's just kids playing..."

"Exactly," Tasya chimed in. "Let's hurry up and go paint the walls."

"They're not just playing," Zhenya objected indecisively. "They're trying to push someone... Into the river."

"Oh come on." Danila took her by the hand. "That's just how it looks to you. Let's go."

He went to drag her along behind, but Zhenya stood firm. For the first time since that night when he had come back, she found his touch unpleasant. His hand seemed too warm somehow, like the plastic case of a tablet slightly overheated by a shoot'em up game.

"We should go and take a look," Zhenya said, breaking free.

"We're not going," Tasya said impudently. "Do what you want, Mum, but we're going home."

"That's not up to you," Zhenya checked her.

To her amazement, Danila didn't help her teach this lesson. On the contrary, as if he was a kid too, he said obligingly: "Home it is then."

Then he added: "I always listen to my little princess."

Until they had disappeared from view, Zhenya watched their backs, feeling a sort of long-forgotten, childish sort of jealousy: as if you're playing Postman's Knock and the boy you like keeps running after your friend, not you.

She wasn't wrong. They really were trying to push him off the concrete wall of the embankment. And even before she could make out his face, for some reason she knew: the "retard." Vinogradov. The reject.

Vinogradov was lying face down on the wall ineffectually fending off his attackers with his feet. His left hand was scrabbling at the smooth, pigeon shit-covered concrete, trying to get a grip on it; his right was hanging down for some reason – as if he was trying to hold someone up above a chasm, as in Hollywood action movies. This pose was so lifelike that the first thing Zhenya did was rush to see whether there really was someone there (and of course there wasn't; Vinogradov's hand had frozen into a tense little spatula, and his emerald green baseball cap was floating in the dark water) and only later did she start pulling the feral children off him.

There were four of them – two boys and two girls; one of the boys was in Tasya's year. They didn't argue, they didn't resist and they didn't try to justify themselves – her intervention was a slight annoyance, nothing more. Silently and obediently they stepped a couple of metres back from Vinogradov – and continued to stand there, their heads tilted to the side, like pigeons waiting for a passer-by to leave so they can calmly return to eating the roadkill that had once been their friend.

Vinogradov clambered on to the dirty tarmac and squatted down, his back resting against the low wall. There was blood and snot coming out of his nose.

"Don't go," he told Zhenya calmly. "If you go they'll start again."

Then he added: "Yegor can't swim."

"Is your name Yegor?" Zhenya didn't know his first name, only his surname. He probably really does have serious difficulties if he's talking about himself in the third person.

"My name is Kolya." Vingradov spread the bloody snot around his chin with his hand.

"So who's Yegor?"

"My friend."

"Was he here too?"

"He's here right now." Vinogradov pointed at the empty tarmac next to him.

Poor boy. He's really very sick.

"Have you no shame?" Zhenya turned to the bullies. It sounded fake somehow, stagey, she herself didn't like how it sounded. "You nasty little creeps," she added. "You monsters." That sounded more natural.

The children continued to stand there in silence. They didn't look at her.

"I know you," she said to the boy from Tasya's form. "I know where you go to school. The rest of you give me your full names right now."

It was her favourite tactic, it worked without fail, especially on nasty little creeps – nurses, guards, shop assistants – "Give me your full name". The fear that all creeps have, unshiftable like old-man sweat, that their name will be put on a list somewhere. Sometimes there was another fear too, a primordial, semi-bestial fear: he who names you owns you, he who masters your secret nickname masters you.

The trick with the name and surname worked: they wandered off in silence. They kept looking back: in case she, satisfied, might just suddenly leave and they could go back. But she didn't leave.

Vinogradov got up and extended her his hand, like an adult. The patches of red were almost gleaming on his fingers – the blood and snot from his nose. Suppressing her disgust, Zhenya shook the sticky hand.

"Let's call your parents," she said.

"My parents have gone." Vinogradov pulled a cheap, battered phone out of his pocket.

"What… they've… they've gone away somewhere?"

Even before Vinogradov answered, shivers covered her neck and back.

"They rejected me."

"So who do you live with?"

Instead of replying, he poked a button on the phone and looked off somewhere in the direction of Interiors. She heard someone's phone chirping behind the trees. And then breaking off.

"Gran, get over here," he said into the receiver and, not waiting for a reply, hung up. "Yegor would like to tell you something." Vinogradov tilted his head to the right, making it seem as if he was listening carefully to someone she couldn't see.

Shivers tickled her spine and chest again with cold, dry little feet. An imaginary friend. She'd read about this problem before.

"Yegor says that, since you've helped us, he will do a good deed for you too."

"Like in a fairy tale?" Zhenya said as gently as possible.

"Like in a fairy tale." Vinogradov was very serious. "You're absolutely right."

An old woman appeared – the same one who had been feeding bread to the pigeons. From up close her wrinkles didn't seem so cheerful. Her waxen face looked as if she'd pressed it against a metal grid while the wax cooled. She grabbed hold of Vinogradov's hand in a business-like way and dragged him toward the pedestrian crossing, making sure not to look at Zhenya. Zhenya followed them awkwardly. They were going the same way, actually.

"Yegor says he should come to your house," Vinogradov turned to her. "Otherwise he won't be able to do you a good deed."

"Quiet, quiet…" the old woman started jabbering. "Don't you go telling no tales."

The old lady's voice was dull and monotonous, as if inside her in her stomach, a worn piece of videotape was unspooling.

"Do you live nearby?" Vinogradov insisted. "Because Yegor and I could come round right now."

Zhenya walked on in silence, tapping out her thoughts with her feet. He's not well. He's crazy. This kid is not our problem. He's not well. He's mad. How do you say no to a lunatic…?

"Don't you tell me no tales..." the old woman started up again. "And don't pester people. You're not a well boy… People won't have you in their house… You're not a well boy…"

She suddenly felt ashamed. Ashamed and disgusted that this harridan was speaking her thoughts out loud. Articulated in this sorrowful old-lady voice they seemed particularly despicable.

"Well I don't know," Zhenya said loudly. "We'd be delighted if Kolya came to see us."

"And Yegor too," Vinogradov said stubbornly.

"Don't you go telling tales."

"I really do think that it would be very nice if Kolya came round," Zhenya said to the old woman.

"He's not a well boy," the old woman said, frightened.

"It's OK. There's nothing to worry about."

## 7

*A demon will turn the fifth fairy's head*
*The fourth will run to the wood to hide*
*The third will hide in the cooking-pot*
*They'll string up the second and tighten the knot.*

(Lullaby)

"Why did you bring him here?" Tasya hissed, when Vinogradov went to wash his hands. "He's a reject!"

"So what?"

"But he's retarded! He wasn't sold a Shhmoochie."

Tasya's face was white with rage. Zhenya had never seen her like this.

"I don't like it one bit when you talk like that. It's not his fault that he's got these problems. We should, in fact, be trying to support him…"

"But they're *his* problems… And you brought him to our house. To our castle. And he… and he…" – Tasya's voice was trembling – "brought someone invisible with him!"

Zhenya struggled to suppress a smile. Tasya really is such a little girl still! It's so touching, this absence of a line between real life and fantasy. She really believes that "someone invisible" has come into their house. She's afraid of this unseen guest and so she's angry… The other kids probably have a go at him for the same reason. They're afraid. They're willing to believe in his craziness.

"Invisible Yegor doesn't exist," Zhenya whispered. "He thinks he can see him, but it's just made up, he believes in it too strongly. But you and I know that really the only other person here is Kolya. And Kolya isn't well, he's got a mental illness, he needs help…"

She went silent: Vinogradov had come back into the kitchen.

"Yegor would like to meet Tasya's daddy."

"My mummy thinks you're crazy," Tasya said smarmily.

He looked at Zhenya with a tired expression that was far from childish, and nodded calmly:

"We know."

"Tea and chocolates!" Zhenya squeaked falsely. "Let's go get Daddy too."

"No he's asleep, don't wake him, don't," Tasya started gabbling.

...She went to get him – but Danila really was asleep: on his back, in his clothes, on top of the made bed. It was strange: normally it was impossible to convince him to go for a lie down in the day, even when he was sick. And he hated sleeping on his back. She leant over him and carefully touched his forehead with her lips – not too hot. If anything, the opposite. Too cold somehow. As if she'd kissed a bit of plastic.

As if he wasn't really alive.

But he was breathing, of course: his chest was rising and falling rhythmically. She opened the window wide: the room had the thick smell of undried paint. The renovations in their bedroom were, it was fair to say, completed. She noticed that Danila had finished off the places where they hadn't had enough Medieval Red Wine. She, Tasya and Danila called their bedroom the ruby hall.

Walls the colour of rubies.

*the colour of blood*

Walls the colour of the wine they would drink from old-fashioned goblets.

*those goblets are, it seems, skull-shaped*

Nausea rose to her throat in biting acid chunks. There was something wrong, there was something unnatural about this room, about this person that was sleeping in it. Whatever it was muddled her thoughts and made her queasy, as if she was driving down a winding road. It was as if it was slightly asymmetrical — there was some barely perceptible error in proportion. The head takes up slightly less room on the flowery pillow than you'd expect. The fingers, slackened in sleep, should be hanging a little differently. The index finger shouldn't be level with the little finger, in a drawing that would be a mistake... The index finger should be set back a little bit, as if it's continuing the palm. And all the shadows... oh God, the shadows are wrong. They should be a touch shorter and the angle's not right...

Zhenya shut her eyes tight. It's not possible. It's completely impossible. It's just her nerves. Something wrong with her eyesight. It'll pass any minute now.

And, in fact, when she opened her eyes, it had got better. Everything's OK. The shadows are shadows. The fingers are fingers. Maybe they really shouldn't have settled on that red-wine colour. It's too aggressive, too loud. It irritates the optic nerve.

She gave Danila a big kiss on the cheek (his cheek was normal, warm even!) and went back to the kids in the kitchen.

Vinogradov and Tasya were sitting in silence at the table and trying hard not to look at each other. Their tea, which smelled like a floor cloth, was getting cold in the ridiculous cups with kittens on them (Tasya had nagged her into buying them a year ago). She'd only brewed it that morning, and it was so fragrant, but now it was as if it had been stewing for a week…

Tasya clutched her Shhmoochie tightly to her tummy, protecting it from any threat. Vinogradov was nonchalantly munching toffees out of a crinkly plastic bag. He had placed three unwrapped sweets on the table to his right, which he didn't touch. For his friend probably.

"Danila's asleep. We'll have our tea without him," Zhenya said.

"Heezh not ashleep." He cradled the sugary beige pulp of the toffee in his mouth. "He jusht doezhn't egzhisht."

"Rubbish!" Tasya screeched and swung her thin, bony hand at Vinogradov. "My daddy does exist!"

"Why don't we go and show Kolya our daddy?" Zhenya intervened, trying to make peace. She regretted bringing this schizophrenic, or whatever he was, into their house.

"No!" Tasya's screech was even more piercing. "We're not going to show him our Daddy! This isn't a zoo!"

Vinogradov smiled a creepy, cretinous smile. The amber toffee syrup had congealed in the corners of his mouth.

"Your Daddy doesn't exist! And this is not a castle! Yegor knows what game you're playing…"

"Get out! Get out! Get out!" Tasya whined. "Mum kick him out! They've both got to leave!"

"Yegor wants to sing you the song about the fairies," Vinogradov announced. "Each fairy will hug her sisters and go-o-o, Together to make a bonfire glo-o-ow, Together their food in a pot they'll se-e-ethe, Together the garden flowers we-e-eave, And into the pond together they'll di-i-ive," he droned, consciously stretching his dirty lips into a grim smile. "A demon will turn the fifth fairy's he-e-ead, The fourth will run to the wood to hi-i-ide, The third will hide in the cooking-po-o-ot, They'll string up the second and tighten the kno-o-ot."

"That's enough!" Zhenya slammed her hand down on the table. "Kolya. Go home."

"Fine," he kept smiling. "But Yegor didn't have time to tell you what your flat *really* looks like. He was only getting started..."

*walls the colour of dried blood and shadows that look wrong*

"Get the hell out!" Zhenya bellowed.

Vinogradov stopped smiling and covered his head with his arm, as if expecting to be hit.

"First I have to call my grandma," he whispered.

Her head went hot with shame. She'd frightened a sick child. She'd shouted at him. She'd lost it. She'd been a mean bitch.

"I'm sorry, Kolya. Of course, let's call your grandma. And you, Tasya, go to your room until I say."

Tasya left in silence, clutching her Shhmoochie.

"Come and pick me up, Grandma," Vinogradov said down the phone and sniffled quietly.

## 8

Within the first few days after purchase a strong
mental bond forms between the child and **Shhmoochie**.
This bond does not harm your offspring;
On the contrary it helps improve their physical,
mental and psychological health.

...The old woman came quickly to pick him up, but it didn't help. Zhenya gave them a handful of toffees and an apple to take with them. She hoped that when the door closed behind the boy everything would go back to how it was before – how it was in the morning, how it was the night before, vibrant and festive. But he left and everything around her was *still tarnished*. It was as if there was a cold draught creeping across the floor. As if a thin crack had formed under the layer of Medieval Red Wine paint – a fragile, barely perceptible thread of emptiness that would soon weave a giant web over all the walls.

As if the smooth transparent film of happiness enveloping Zhenya had been torn. And everything outside it was cold and harsh.

Their house was cold – she closed the window in the bedroom, but the draught was still there.

Danila was cold – he had woken up in a bad mood and spent the whole evening watching TV, giving monosyllabic replies to her questions.

Their daughter was cold and harsh too – she sat in her room, the door shut, absorbed in her Shhmoochie, and when Zhenya came to tell her dinner was ready she snapped at her rudely:

"You should really knock."

"It's really up to me," Zhenya said angrily, "whether I knock or not. I make the rules in this house."

"And Daddy," Tasya quietly added.

"Yes. And Daddy." Zhenya made a poker face.

"And Daddy says that you have to knock if you want to come into my room."

Zhenya felt a wave of cold rage sweep from her stomach to her head, then crash against her throat and then her eyes, not with tears but with something like crushed glass. Rolling this glass on her tongue and then swallowing it down, she said in a nasty trembling voice: "Daddy's been away for too long to be telling me what I 'have' to do. Is that clear? Is that clear?"

Tasya nodded indifferently.

"I have decided," Zhenya said, putting the emphasis on the "I", "that from now on the door to your room is going to be open at all times. Is that clear?"

"No," Tasya replied.

"What exactly is not clear?" Zhenya said tersely, hating herself for the military tone she was taking. You shouldn't talk to your child like that. You mustn't.

"Nothing." Tasya calmly swirled her finger across the screen of her Shhmoochie. "But my door has got to be closed."

"It is not *your* door!" Zhenya screeched.

Tasya carefully lay her Shhmoochie on the table as if it was a crystal dish, then got up, went over to the door and shut it right in Zhenya's face. Not fast, not slamming it, just closing it calmly, with a clear sense of her own self-worth.

It wasn't the action itself, but this calmness that really infuriated Zhenya. It transformed her into a crazed, hairy macaque, swinging through the trees, breaking branches with her arms, trying to throw her own child to the ground.

Although, in actual fact, she never touched Tasya. All she did was knock the door open with her shoulder, charge into Tasya's room, grab the Shhmoochie from her hands and fling it hard against the wall; the screen went fuzzy, bits of plastic scattered over the floor… But she never touched her daughter, never. Literally: she hadn't even gone near her. Let alone pushed her or hit her. Which made what happened next even harder to watch.

Tasya fell over – she was just sitting there, and then suddenly she fell, hitting her temple against the corner of her desk. She buried her face in the gold-spattered wooden floor and just lay there. "Can we, Mummy? In our palace I want my room to be the gold one." The memory came to Zhenya out of nowhere. She looked at Tasya lying there motionless and for a few long, endless seconds she didn't know what she was supposed to do or what was even happening. She saw everything through some sort of veil of steam – as if she was cut off from Tasya by a shower curtain covered in rivulets of moisture. And even when Zhenya's eyes and head had cleared and she went over to her daughter, it was as if she could feel the slimy touch of this strange barrier on Tasya's cheeks and neck.

She took Tasya into her arms and laid her down on the sofa. She felt her pulse – thank God – and listened to her breathing: even. There was no evident damage to her face, not a single drop of blood. But she was unconscious. And pale. Terrifyingly pale. The thought crossed her mind that in these cases a slap to the face can help – but she hurriedly rejected that idea. She wasn't going hit her own child. Particularly not on the face. Particularly not when she's unconscious. A sort of sleepy, heavy dullness overcame her once again. Her daughter is lying there unconscious. What should she do…? Where's Danila…?

She went, like a sleepwalker, into the bedroom. Danila wasn't there – not in the bedroom, not anywhere. She didn't remember when and where he had gone. Had he said goodbye? *there's something important*, something she needs to do right now. But Danila's gone… *there's something* It's hard to remember what's important when there's wriggly little worm gnawing into the flesh of your darkening happiness. When there are questions banging against your head like rotten apples: what if he's gone for a long time again, gone for good? *there's something urgent*. And what if he never comes back again? And that hopeless, lonesome howl-at-the-moon anguish returns? And you're a single mother again. Alone with your child. *With your child who's lying motionless on the floor…* Oh God, it's urgent. She suddenly remembered what she needed to do *right now* and hurried to call the ambulance.

## 9

The materials your **Shhmoochie** is made from are waterproof, flameproof and shockproof.

"Her condition is very serious." He scrunched up his face in disapproval.

"Are you responsible for this?"

"What do you mean?" Zhenya yet again adjusted the blanket on top of Tasya, which was sitting quite normally anyway and not slipping off, because Tasya was not moving. She understood what he meant but the accusation was so absurd that there was simply no place for it in her mind.

"What I mean is: did you do this to your daughter?"

"I would never hit my daughter," Zhenya said colourlessly, as if she were reading what she needed to say from some invisible autocue. "I don't use corporal punishment. She fell. And hit the corner of the desk. And lost consciousness. What should we do? Tell me what we should do? Are you going to take her to hospital?"

"'She fell'," the doctor mimicked her. "And there you are smelling of roses. The ambulance is going to come, deal with it, fix everything – that's what you think isn't? Isn't it? And this here..." he nodded at the Shhmoochie lying on the floor. "Am I supposed to fix this too?!"

This was all so weird that Zhenya emerged from her bitter sadness, like a drowning man swimming up from the bottom of a cold pool, and gave a nervous giggle.

"What's her Shhmooochie got to do with anything?" she picked the gadget up off the floor along with the pieces that had fallen off. "Why are you going on about my daughter's Shhmoochie instead of helping her? Right then, give me your full name. I'm going to write a letter of complaint."

"By all means." The spell hadn't worked. "Yakov Koganovich. And as for letters of complaint – I'll be writing one about you. And passing it on to the relevant authorities. This is a typical case of deliberate harm. So don't go thinking you can get it fixed under warranty! She wants to try and scare me...! You're going to have to pay for it all yourself, understand? The warranty doesn't cover cases like this. 'She fell'!... You should think for a second before you go wrecking something...!

"What are you... what warranty?! What are you on about?"

He's crazy. He's not going to help Tasya. He's an absolute lunatic. They're losing precious time. And why's he here on his own, without a paramedic? Where's his stethoscope, where's his first aid kit?!

"Who exactly are you!?" Zhenya squealed, but immediately checked herself: you've got to be calm when dealing with crazy people. She asked curtly: "What hospital does your ambulance operate out of?"

"Not from any hospital," Koganovich replied grumpily. "Your call was rerouted to Nannyland. Typical complaints. Typical symptoms. Standard in instances of damage to the unit or software."

Koganovich stood up and took the Shhmoochie and the two broken parts from Zhenya's hands. She didn't try to stop him. She felt as if the slightest movement might make the world crack and fall apart so she should just freeze and not move a muscle. Like Tasya.

Muttering to himself, Koganovich set about putting one of the broken bits of plastic back into the Shhmoochie.

Still trying not to move, Zhenya said:

"My daughter needs help."

"Of course she does," Koganovich nodded, not looking up from the Shhmoochie.

"And you're playing with that toy."

"I actually happen to be giving your daughter first aid, do you understand, woman?"

Woman, Zhenya repeated in her head. It sounds biblical. And he created woman from the rib of… Or, no, it's the opposite, it's scientific: all she is is a female, the rest doesn't matter. Understand, *woman*. But she didn't understand. Stupid cow.

"I don't understand."

Koganovich looked up from the Shhmoochie and catapulted the prickly bushes of his eyebrows into his upper forehead, expressing something that was either surprise or horror.

"Did you even read the Shhmoochie manual, woman? You did sign the contract, right? Point six, safety – both in the manual and in the contract. It's all written there clearly, for the alternatively gifted." Koganovich rolled his eyes and started reciting from memory in a boring voice. "In the first few days after purchase a strong mental bond forms between the child and Shhmoochie. This bond does not harm your offspring; on the contrary, it helps improve their physical, mental and psychological health. Sudden or violent interruptions of this bond can be associated with serious threats to their health and can even be fatal. For this reason we strongly recommend that your Shhmoochie games console is protected from all possible causes of damage (breaking, dropping, scratching, water damage, replacement parts, exposure to a naked flame). If such damage does occur, your child may experience complications (including, if the Shhmoochie is entirely inoperative, coma). The Nannyland Corporation is not liable for the life or health of your offspring in the event of deliberate damage to the games console. Nevertheless, it should be noted that the materials that Shhmoochie is made of are waterproof, flameproof and shockproof, which make it almost impossible to render it entirely inoperative."

Koganovich grunted studiously as he fixed a part to the inside of the Shhmoochie.

"I'm going to try and start it up in safe mode," he said. "But there's been serious damage to the software. You should be prepared for some outages – and a lot of games and programmes will be missing. At some point in the next two days you have to go to the Nannyland office where you bought the Fairy Rosie and pay to have it repaired. It is not necessary to take the Shhmoochie in to the office, understand, woman? Repairs will be carried out remotely. For your daughter: bed rest. And plenty of liquids."

He went over to Tasya and put the Shhmoochie down on the chair next to her. The screen lit up – it was very murky, not like the normal screen, but still. Something crunched away unhappily inside.

"It's loading," Koganovich noted, very proud of himself.

"She's unconscious," Zhenya said bluntly. "How is she going to be able to drink?"

"She'll regain consciousness," Koganovich yawned.

Tasya coughed and opened her eyes.

## 10

Hello-hello!
I'm your Fairy Rose, I've woken up again!
If I fall asleep, it won't be for long, don't worry.
I'll be with you forever, I promise.

**Shhmoochie**. More than just a game.
Together forever.

For the rest of the evening, Tasya kept emerging from her strange slumber and then plunging back into it. Another doctor came to see her (Zhenya paid for one from a private clinic to come) but he confirmed – very politely and sadly – what Koganovich had said. A mental bond. Repairs needed. No other treatment available. Sees a lot of cases like this.

Her thoughts tumbled round, heavy and somehow numb, as if she was coming round from a trance. She tried to feel angry. What's going on here? She should sue that Nannyland. Doing this to kids.

But there was no anger. And no sense of indignation. Just the unending desire to atone for her crime – and the fear that she wouldn't get that chance.

Danila came back, and for some reason said the same thing as Koganovich:

"You are responsible."

Then he went off somewhere again. She thought: yes, I am. I have sinned.

When Tasya regained consciousness, she was lying hugging her Shhmoochie and stroking its smooth pink case – the fairies, their hair, their faces. She ran her finger over the screen, trying to reanimate some important game or other. She seemed sad and slightly groggy – but she didn't seem to be cross with Zhenya. Actually, she didn't seem to care. Zhenya sat next to her on the bed, held her hand, read her a book, gave her tea with lemon, mint and sugar. Not long ago Tasya had liked being ill because it meant she would get her monthly ration of attention "in bulk". Now it seemed as if she didn't notice that Zhenya was there with her. She quietly drew her hand out of Zhenya's so it would be easier to hug her Shhmoochie. She didn't listen to Zhenya when she was reading, she didn't laugh in the right places. She drank her sweet tea obediently, but didn't notice the taste.

She just wanted to be with her Fairy Rosie – nothing else mattered. And when "Rosie" suddenly shimmered then went black and shut down (and that happened practically every hour), she would stick it deep under her pillow, close her eyes and instantly shut down too.

"Sleep, little one," Zhenya said, but she knew: Tasya wasn't sleeping. When you're sleeping your face doesn't go so white. Your nose doesn't get so sharp.

Zhenya spent all evening calling the Nannyland office, it was engaged, finally she got through, told them about the "accidental breakage." The girl on the phone immediately changed her tone and became very unfriendly, but Zhenya sucked up to her and kept apologising. In the end she was given permission to come in in the morning and pay for the repairs – which, the girl promised, would take no more than 24 hours. It was far from cheap, but that didn't matter, of course.

After that she didn't feel quite so bad. The next day she'd go and get everything fixed. While Tasya *slept* (Zhenya still tried to use that word in her head), she couldn't concentrate on anything – she just sat on the internet and searched for similar incidents. She found a lot. She read blogs and forums, drenched in sweat; several times she got into a terrible panic, but just as often she felt an incredible sense of relief. Everyone's story started either badly or very badly.

*i dropped shhmoochie – now my daughter has problems talking*

*i threw that bloody game out the window now my son can't walk*

*scratched*

*thrown in the bin*

*hidden*
*broken*
*pain syndrome*
*short of breath*
*losing consciousness*
*in a coma*

...but they always ended well. The Nannyland Corporation were efficient in carrying out repairs. The day after the payment all of the Shhmoochies started working again without outages, all the kids felt fantastic and everyone lived happily ever after.

There was not a single negative review of Nannyland. Although everyone happily slagged off something called "unlocking".

*In my personal opinion you're always better off going down the official route or you might get sold a pup*

*Don't be stupid avoid conmen trying to sell you unlocking*

...Later, towards midnight, Tasya came round again and went on her Shhmoochie: she really wanted to play her favourite lullaby, the one about the fairies. At first the programme wouldn't load, and Tasya started this thin, pitiful snivelling, like a one-year old, and Zhenya offered to sing her the song about the little lamb instead, but Tasya shook her head and refused... and then, when they'd given up hope, when Tasya's snivelling was starting to turn into a proper tantrum, the screen suddenly blinked and a gentle woman's voice – a voice perfect for consoling a sick, crying child – said:

"Five fairy sisters"

Then pipes, fiddle and crystal bells

"*... Each fairy will hug her sisters and go*
*Together to make a bonfire glow...*"

Zhenya kissed Tasya on the forehead, then on the tip of her nose and got up.

"*Together their food in a pot they'll seethe*
*Together the garden flowers weave*
*And into the pond together they'll dive.*
*...*"

"Close the door, Mummy," Tasya asked weakly.

"Out of the question. You are seriously ill and I have to be able to see you and hear you."

It didn't sound right. It sounded too harsh, too much like an ultimatum.

You shouldn't talk to sick children like that. You should talk to them in the same honey-soft, consoling voice as Shhmoochie…

"It'll be better if the door is open, little one," she automatically tried to imitate Shhmoochie's cooing, but it sounded fake. Like a line said by a second-rate actress playing a two-faced stepmother in a Mexican movie.

Tasya closed her eyes and said nothing in reply.

*"A demon will turn the fifth fairy's head*
*The fourth will run to the wood to hide*
*The third will hide in the garden there*
*The second will sense disaster's near*
*They'll drown the first in the murky mere..."*

Zhenya sat at her desk and flicked through a magazine deliberately loudly, rustling and crackling the pages. She didn't want Tasya to think she was listening to the song coming from her room. She really would rather not have listened to that awful song. But the door was open – and she could hear it. She could hear every sonorous crystal word.

*"A demon will turn the fifth fairy's head*
*The fourth will run to the wood to hide*
*The third will hide in the cooking-pot*
*They'll string up the second and tighten the knot.*

*A demon will turn the fifth fairy's head*
*The fourth will run to the wood to hide*
*The third will weep for the one that's gone*
*And on the fire her body they'll burn.*

*A demon will turn the fifth fairy's head*
*The fourth will run to the wood to hide*
*She'll breakfast where the trees are cool*
*And be poisoned by a black toadstool.*

*The fifth fairy, left all alone*
*Will rescue the first where she sank like a stone*
*From the second one's neck she'll remove the mark*
*And collect the third from ashes dark*
*Give the fourth some stock to ease her pain*

*And then there'll be five of them again.*
*Each fairy will hug her sisters and go*
*Together to make a bonfire glow...*"

It never ended, that damned song. It flowed and circled round, always going back to the beginning. Like the rantings of a madman, like feverish blood in your veins, like a drowning man in a whirlpool. Around and around.

"*Together the garden flowers weave*
*And into the pond together they'll dive.*
*A demon will turn the fifth fairy's head...*"

These words, the way they kept circling back round, made Zhenya dizzy and cold and she could feel a pressure under her ribs on the left. As if, below her heart, in the place where she had once carried her daughter, there was now a hard, coarse spinning snowball, and with every revolution it kept growing and growing, pressing against her... These words made it impossible to breathe – and so did the words in black next to her pictures in the magazine.

She'd flicked through it many times, this issue. She'd read the story about the elf-psychologist quite a few times. At first before when she was doing the illustrations, then afterwards. How could she not have noticed? How could she not have *compared* them?

"'You're so beautiful,' Arkady whispered passionately, pressing his lips against her hair and breathing in their scent hungrily. 'Don't kick me out, I beg you. I can't live without you. Without you both. Please let me stay.'"

"'I kept this T-shirt because it reminded me of home. I missed you so much.'"

"'It's so good to be home.'"

"'I always obey my little princess.'"

All these words, and dozens more, hundreds more which Danila had said to her since coming back home. None of them are his. All these glossy words belong to someone else...

She suddenly realised that she had no idea whether Danila was home or not. He'd appeared and disappeared a few times that evening and that night. Whenever he appeared...

*like a ghost*

...he'd go in and see Tasya, float around somewhere in her peripheral vision and bang plates in the kitchen, but he didn't talk to her once

*like a ghost, a ghost*

She got so scared that she ran into the bedroom (he was there, sleeping, his face buried in the pillow), turned on all the lights, shook him, said they needed to talk.

He was completely groggy – as anyone would be when they've just been woken up. He sat up in bed. His eyes were blank, like shiny round buttons with a dark point in the middle. He rubbed them with his fingers, in a circular motion, as if he was cleaning them. He unstuck his lips with a saliva-filled smack:

"After what you've done, it's hard for me to talk to you."

*bingo*

The snowball in her chest started spinning three times quicker, then broke free and slipped down to somewhere below her stomach. A character in the story, a Byronic fifty-something with no job (but who later gets rich), used that phrase to his cheating bitch of a wife (who later cleans up her act).

"Can you say the same thing using different words?"

He stared at her darkly – with no look of surprise, with no expression at all. Calmly, as if examining a badly done picture in a magazine, she noticed that Danila didn't have a shadow. But that very second, as if some invisible artist had just taken the critique on board, a shadow popped out and stuck to the wall like a flattened, dark crimson tadpole.

*he's not sleeping he just doesn't exist*

The paint's not even, Zhenya thought for some reason. It's not even, the paint has dried in lumps.

*yegor knows what game you're playing*

"You're not here," Zhenya said and closed her eyes.

"You're crazy." Danila started pulling on his trousers. "It's only pity that keeps me from leaving you."

That phrase hadn't been used by the guy with no job, but, quite the opposite, by a banker. The unfaithful husband of one of the elf-psychiatrist's patients. Then he got better too. Because they all got better.

She didn't open her eyes until she heard the door slam in the corridor.

*yegor knows what game you're playing*

## 11

Sick and tired of the lack of trust and togetherness in your family?
Sick and tired of everything being decided for you?
Are you fed up with some corporation taking liberties

and playing with your offspring like a puppet on a string?
Do you want to have control over your offspring
and play a full role in your child's life?

*Unlocking. Cheap. Quick. Reliable. We accept all models of Shhmoochie.*

"And where's your little Totsie?" Maria shot Zhenya an anxious look. "You don't look well, Yevgenia."

The gaggle of clucking and cooing mothers suddenly fell silent – as if they'd seen a bird of a different feather.

"Tasya is a little unwell," Zhenya chirruped as light-heartedly as possible. "And I'm a bit short on sleep."

Maria narrowed her deranged eyes:

"And everything is OK with your Shhmoochie?"

"Everything's wonderful." Zhenya automatically rubbed her bag strap. In the bag was the envelope with the necessary fee. She'd take the envelope to Nannyland and everything would be fine. They'll fix it. Everything will go back to normal and be absolutely fine. She shouldn't have come here – she should have gone straight to Nannyland. And what happened last night... What she thought she saw last night was a panic attack, these things happen. When you're worried and you're not sleeping, these things happen. She shouldn't have come here, to the school...

"Children rarely get ill if their Shhmoochie is in working order," said Tasya's form teacher, who was standing there in the midst of the flock. She was wearing a white dress with lace detailing that clung to her flabby arse. Why isn't she in class...?

"How right you are, Miss Mikhailova!" Sukhodolskaya squealed ecstatically.

"I'm worried about Tasya," Miss Mikhailova said in a metallic voice. "We're all worried about her."

"You should be more worried about the fact that lessons have already started and you're standing here yakking away," Zhenya barked.

Miss Mikhailova batted her eyes, like a doll that's been laid flat and then put upright again.

"You'd do well to know, Yevgenia," Maria intervened reproachfully, "that our kiddies have been looking after themselves for some time now. Shhmoochie has a learn-together programme, you know, which not only helps to encourage teamwork but also sets a certain standard..."

The old woman turned up at the school gates with Vinogradov. They stopped. She was mumbling something non-stop. He said nothing and didn't look at her. She gave him a little shove. He started shaking his head. She whacked him. He fended it off with his arm. She hooked onto his arm and dragged him onto the school grounds. He said something. She let him go. He set off slowly on his own. She disappeared behind the gates. The whole scene looked like a well-rehearsed clown act.

"Yevgenia, you're not listening… If this is of no interest to you…"

"I'm interested," Zhenya slowly started walking over to intercept Vinogradov.

"Retard…" The mothers' voices started rustling away behind her.

She shouldn't, she shouldn't. She shouldn't talk to him. She should just go.

"Leave me alone!" Vinogradov recoiled. "I'll get my grandma."

"Kolya, I need to talk to you," Zhenya said, very quietly, so the mothers wouldn't hear her.

"Yegor and I don't want to talk. You kicked us out."

"Sorry… Sorry. I was wrong. Please, Kolya."

"No," he tried to walk past her.

"But what about the good deed? Remember, like in a fairy tale? The reward for sticking up for you…"

"Yegor says that you didn't give him a chance to do the good deed. Now he doesn't owe you anything."

"But couldn't you… couldn't you and Yegor just talk to me anyway, just because? What did you mean when you said that Tasya's daddy doesn't exist? Please, it's important. It's just… something's happened at home. I broke her Shhmoochie."

Vinogradov narrowed his eyes – in an unkind, grown-up way – and tilted his head to the side. Then he nodded and looked at Zhenya with a crooked smile:

"Nothing happens just because. Especially in fairy tales. But if you do what we ask, we will answer three questions."

"OK," Zhenya agreed. "What do I have to do?"

What nonsense. Why play silly games with a sick child…

"Say, really loud, so everyone can hear you: 'I broke the damn Shhmoochie'!"

"Why?!"

"Let's just say it's so that Yegor can have a bit of fun."

"No. I'm not going to do that."

"Suit yourself," Vinogradov took a quick look around and set off back towards the school gates.

"You're not going to lessons?"

"You really haven't understood anything, have you? There are no lessons."

"Then what is there?" Zhenya said dumbly.

"Toys."

"What toys?"

"Toys like your Tasya."

She watched Vinogradov leaving, and behind her the mothers watched her watching.

"Yevgenia, you're frightening us. Why did you talk to him?"

"...He's a reject you know."

"...He needs to be isolated."

"...His type are dangerous for people like us, and our kids."

*toys like your Tasya*

She turned to the gaggle.

"And what are we like?"

The mothers looked at each other.

"We are people whose lives have been enriched by Nannyland," Miss Mikhailova said in a resonant, triumphant voice, like a school prefect. "People who have Shhmoochie."

"Shhmoochie brings everyone happiness," Maria barked back.

"Shhmoochie. Changing the world for the better."

"Shhmoochie. Bringing happiness home."

"Shhmoochie. More than just a game."

"Now you," Miss Mikhailova said, touching Zhenya on the shoulder. "Feel that joy. Say something nice about Shhmoochie! Go on? Shhmoochie..." she smiled expectantly. "Shhmoochie..."

"I broke the damn Shhmoochie," Zhenya said.

Vinogradov was waiting for her outside the school fence.

"Three questions," he said in a business-like manner. "And be quick about it."

Her head was buzzing. Her thoughts were knocking into each other, banging into an invisible barrier like bugs in a jar.

"Why were you not sold Shhmoochie?" Zhenya blurted out.

"A silly question," Vinogradov said. "But Yegor said that that's normal. In fairy tales they always start with some silly, pointless question... I wasn't sold Shhmoochie because of Yegor. Because they need children that are unoccupied so they can play in there quietly, and I'm already kind of taken. That monster said I already belong to someone. But that's not true. Yegor and I are friends, he's not my owner, we have equal..."

"What… monster?"

"That's your second question. And it's not such a silly one. But Yegor and I don't know the answer. All we know is that those monsters that sell Shhmoochie and then use it to control people – they are definitely not people. Perhaps they're aliens." Vinogradov absent-mindedly stuck a finger in his nostril. "Or, you know, robots…"

"You said that Danila doesn't exist."

"A question?"

"Danila, my husband. Tasya's daddy. Who… What is he?"

"He's nothing. That is, somewhere he probably really does exist, or maybe he's died, we don't know anything about that. But he hasn't come back. Yegor says that he's not in your house. He's just part of the game about the magical fairy. He was created by Tasya. She is learning to build things that are more and more complicated as the player takes her up on to higher levels. That was your last question."

"What am I supposed to do?!"

"You've already asked three questions. Yegor is tired. He wants to go for a walk. He doesn't want to tell you how to deal with the monster."

"You're a monster," Zhenya whispered. "You're mentally ill, you're a monster!"

"You've hurt Yegor's feelings," Kolya said. "He's never going to help you again."

Vinogradov pulled out a brownish bogie, examined it thoroughly, then rolled it into a ball in his fingers. Again he studied it carefully, like an Etruscan seer reading omens in an animal's entrails, and popped it in his mouth.

"Something's going to happen today," he said and made a swallowing motion. "Today you're going to get led astray."

She watched him walking away clumsily, holding hands with the emptiness that was his friend.

## 12

"We understand your concern, but the product cannot be exchanged or returned," trilled a girl in a pinky-gold fairy costume and an iridescent kerchief.

"I don't need the money," Zhenya said. "You don't have to return the money. If you like I'll throw this in too," she shook the envelope. "Just take my daughter off your system!"

"What system?" the sales-girl said in surprise. A lock of hair, white and dry, scorched with peroxide, tumbled out from under her headscarf. "What do you mean 'take her off'? In the first few days after purchase a strong mental bond forms between the child and..."

"I've already heard that."

"...This bond does not harm your offspring..."

"Can you just shut up?" Zhenya shrieked. "You robot! You bloody doll! Give me back my child! Give me back my child, my daughter — normal, as she should be!"

"The product cannot be returned," the fairy said calmly. "Your behaviour is inappropriate. You condition is unstable." She tucked the lock back into the headscarf. "We are obliged to take measures."

There was something about that gesture that was at once both soft and mechanical. Something in that pose. Not the words, no, but the fact that she moved like a 3D animation – that was the final straw. Zhenya gripped the fairy's resplendent headscarf and tore it from her head. She grabbed her by her hair, by those dry white tresses. She pulled with all her might. She wanted to hear plastic snapping, the sound of ripping threads. She wanted to tear this doll's head off, to pull out the cotton wool, or the foam rubber or polystyrene balls or whatever she was stuffed with, and throw it all over the Nannyland office...

There really was a snapping noise – a scarcely audible electronic click. A wave of pain came down her arm, down both arms, and across her body, spreading down to her feet and then shooting back up, into her solar plexus, her oesophagus, her throat, her gums and her teeth.

A guard appeared. Squeamishly, he took Zhenya by the shoulder with two fingers and led her out onto the street.

"Have a nice day, we look forward to seeing you again at Nannyland soon," the fairy said as she left.

Her mouth tasted of metal and spoiled meat, as if she'd been licking a rusty dustbin. She wandered to the metro. She had a lump in her throat, one she couldn't manage to swallow. On the way into the underpass someone pushed her. Then again.

"Unlocking? Unlocking?"

A fidgety, mangy-looking guy with a sign saying "All devices repaired" swinging on his chest and a black ringbinder in his hands looked Zhenya in the eye insistently; as soon as he caught her gaze, he started leafing through the binder. Scanned photographs flashed by in plastic wallets with big red captions — "BEFORE" and "AFTER". The "befores" featured children with sickly, malevolent faces sitting on their own and staring blankly at the screens of their Shhmoochies. The "afters" had the same children, holding the same Shhmoochies, but now they were pink-cheeked and cheerful and hugging their equally pink-cheeked parents.

"Unlocking," the little guy murmured again. "Unlocking. If you've got the cash."

Zhenya tightened her grip on the bag with the envelope inside and sped up. The mangy guy hurried after her down the underpass.

"Unlocking in 24 hours... Any model... Any condition... I'm a father myself... I've got a large family... What else can we do, woman... Parents like us are in a hopeless situation... No court'll touch 'em... Ain't that right, woman...? There's no regulation... What have we got left...? The only option left is unlocking, on the quiet ... But it's done properly! And remotely! And the quality's second to none...!"

## 13

*Together their food in a pot they'll seethe*
*Together the garden flowers weave*
*And into the pond together they'll dive.*

She was in an excellent mood. While she was in the metro, a thought had suddenly struck her: why don't they get a cat? And right there, as if to order, she had come across an old woman in an underpass, wrapped up in an unseasonably woolly coat and holding a basket with a poor little tabby kitten in it. Both the kitten and the old woman had pus weeping out of their eyes.

"How much does he cost?" Zhenya asked.

"I just want him to go to a good home. Enjoy."

...The flat smelled of DIY and something stale. The paint had congealed on the walls in brownish scabs. Up by the ceiling a troupe of flies danced in a circle.

"And this is our castle," Zhenya said to the kitten. "We're going to have to redo everything."

The kitten sneezed and pissed on her shoe.

Tasya was sleeping in her room, cuddled up in a ball around her Shhmoochie. Danila was sitting at the kitchen table, not moving, his back straight.

"Go away," Zhenya told him calmly. "Even if you're real, go away and don't come back."

"You're making a mistake," Danila replied, using the next vaguely familiar phrase. "Why deny yourself happiness when it's so easy?"

"We'll be happy without you." Zhenya tried to wipe one of the kitten's eyes (one of them turned out to have a corneal ulcer), but it hissed and squirmed out of her hands.

"Shhmoochie is the answer to all your problems. Shhmoochie brings happiness home," Danila said.

"Get out of here," Zhenya said. "Tasya is mine."

"The product cannot be returned," Danila said in a crystal-clear woman's voice. There were golden planets embroidered on his T-shirt.

"You're dead." Zhenya closed her eyes. She imagined him getting up and leaving. The door slamming in the corridor.

The door slammed in the corridor. She opened her eyes and went to Tasya's room. The screen of her Rosie shone silver.

"It's working," Tasya smiled. "Look, Mummy, it's working."

She stroked Tasya's head, then ran her finger over the case of the Shhmoochie, which was warm from Tasya's body. Now everything's going to be different. It's going to be a whole new game. They're going to think up the rules together. They'll write beautiful new songs. And the door will always be open.

The kitten came in and jumped on Tasya's duvet. Its eyes were big, clear, green, enchanted.